The Assault

on Tony's

The Assault on Tony's

by John O'Brien

GROVE
PRESS
New York

Published simultaneously in Canada
Printed in the United States of America

FIRST PAPERBACK EDITION

Library of Congress Cataloging-in-Publication Data

O'Brien, John.
    The assault on Tony's / by John O'Brien.
       p.   cm.
     ISBN 0-8021-3542-0
     I. Title.
    PS3565.B669A9   1996
    813'.54—dc20   96-1917

DESIGN BY LAURA HAMMOND HOUGH

Grove Press
841 Broadway
New York, NY 10003

98 99 00 10 9 8 7 6 5 4 3 2 1

The Assault

on Tony's

Day16

"How bad is it?" Langston wanted to know, and the truth was Rudd couldn't tell him.

"Not so bad," he lied.

"Then where's Miles? Not so bad my ass! If it's not so bad then where the hell is Miles? He's down already, isn't he? I should go down before Miles. You know that. So where is he?"

"Only shot," Rudd told him. "Miles got hit last night during the bombing. That's where he is."

Langston eased slightly at this news. "Damn if this thing doesn't have me feeling six ways of fucked. I'll try to keep it together. Really, I will. Sorry, Rudd," he mumbled.

It rattled Rudd to hear Langston cave in—the man had been through a lot without showing the strain that boiled under the rest of them—but he was right. He would have gone down before Miles. He would have been the one to go down first, before any of them. That's why Rudd couldn't tell him how bad it was. And it was bad. It was very bad.

Langston pulled a somber beat, said of his fallen comrade, "Shot. Who knows, maybe it'll make it easier on him."

"I don't think so. He was only hit in the shoulder. I think he even managed to stop the bleeding."

"The bleeding," he echoed, and it seemed he would leave it at that.

But a chuckle rose from behind the perspiration glistening across his forehead, rose beyond the already moderate quaking of his chest. Langston stood up carefully, as if not to frighten off his skittish smile, and his chair fell away like maybe it was thinking now would be a good time to get the hell out of there. "Tell me you didn't sterilize it," he said, his trembling hand seeking out that awesome and feckless bar.

Rudd picked up the laughter, and that made it real laughter. Rudd knew this was part of it, this sort of hopeless mirth. So did Langston. Of course Langston knew. It made him laugh more, under Rudd's painful gaze, now off, away, down.

For another look in what he ironically still referred to in his own head as *dry*-storage, he would best take along a witness. Who would be good he wasn't yet sure. Not Jill, somebody else, one of the guys, and the *dry* in dry-storage was ironic now for obvious reasons, and originally ironic for insignificant reasons. Only that it was the first place he ever kissed a grown woman, so not Jill.

Not Tony's dry-storage, not considering he was thirty-eight the first time he ever stepped into Tony's much less Tony's dry-storage. No, Rudd's first kiss was in one of those godforsaken midwestern cities that last he heard was experiencing only pockets of unrest (would be the phrase) and keeping things more or less under control, one of those places that could provide one with a glimmer of hope provided one looked closely yet not close enough. Rudd was sixteen and bussing tables in a tony restaurant where even the dishwashers

were Caucasian and the busboys were damn near transparent.
So that was that place and it worked so sue him and fuck you
if you don't like it. Worked then and there, anyway.

Prince of that place, and fast, and everybody liked Rudd,
especially this waitress. Gail, it was. Now Rudd's good
enough that he handles the whole place by himself and still
has time to wolf down the occasional untouched order of
scallops while washing it down with a stashed bottle of house
wine rejected by some local goon who thought such a move
might impress his date but didn't know that you've lost your
shot at impressing anybody the moment the phrase *house wine*
crosses your lips. Well Rudd doesn't mind one bit 'cause that
wine tastes just fine back there behind the biggest stainless-
steel sink this rich boy ever wants to get next to. Now Gail's
digging him and likely nipping at whatever gets her through
her own particular night, so she grabs his hand and takes him
into dry-storage, which is the storeroom in the back of the
place for canned goods, rice, flour . . . hence the name.
Close the door and this woman who has probably eight years
on him which may not sound like much but is half again his
age gives him a tonsil licking that would make an oral surgeon
blush. Yet Rudd is less than impressed, like that wine guy's
date, so much so that when poor old wrong-side-of-the-tracks
Gail grabs what she expects to be his hard-on she finds only a
great big piece of humble pie. That was Gail. And Rudd knew
for a fact, his dad used to fuck waitresses, maids.

That story he remembered the first time he walked into
Tony's dry-storage, which was some time after first walking
into Tony's (which, it turns out, was something of a seminal

event in its own right). Sitting at the top of the steps, deciding whom to take back down for a second awful look, Rudd remembered the irony, the utter lack of anything dry in Tony's dry-storage, which of course was filled strictly with liquor. Tony's, a damn fine restaurant, was still primarily a bar, and what was originally bona fide dry-storage soon, Rudd later learned, turned out to be a more appropriate space for the rather formidable back stock of liquor. By then though the room *was* dry-storage, at least to the staff. And now, what with the shutters bolted down and him inside more or less permanently, wasn't Rudd once again on staff at a restaurant? The battle outside raging, one might say, the storage down here much further from dry than it was yesterday, or less so, one might say if one had the courage, what was Rudd if not a de facto employee of Tony's? Or even the boss. Or manager, Rudd thought, that's what I am, Dad, a restaurant manager. And he'd fucked a waitress too. Now didn't that beat all?

Rudd felt the anticipatory withdrawals nipping from inside his abdomen. Also at the back of his neck. And his arms, the backs of his upper arms. This was the sort of thing that kept a less experienced man mired deep in a couch-ridden binge, he knew. He'd been that man—most of them had, certainly Langston—back before Tony's and his second marriage, back before he got *better*. In those days he would mistake this stuff for Big Trouble and hit the vodka bottle prematurely. Now he knew better; he had some time, the condition of dry-storage notwithstanding. Langston was closer though, by at least a day, maybe two.

He felt the ridges in the piece of aluminum that covered the edge of this top step. It was worn less on the sides, the ridges still discernible by eye or by buttock, sobering buttock. Even a screw, unless it was a piece of pocket lint, made its presence known, and this was really going too far, feeling far more than a man in his condition ought to be feeling, a portentous sign. The black steps down to dry-storage each had a worn, bone-colored center from where countless Nikes and Red Wing work shoes had made their marks, or, more accurately, erased another's. Only the top and bottom steps bore aluminum armor, like: you're there, this is as high as it gets, low as it gets, so don't fuck with me 'cause I've seen it all. But Rudd once noticed the bottom piece of aluminum kicked out of place, exposing a bone-colored center like on all the rest of the steps, as if the bottom step had once seen service in the mediocracy, a more central location, the infantry above.

He rested his chin in his right hand, elbow to knee, and reached with his left hand for the handrail at his shoulder, not so much to give himself rise as to advance by just one frame, pause and examine the moment he was in. That rail wobbled when he clutched it, the brass-colored bracket that held it to the wall being fastened with a screw whose anchor was losing its grip. As he grasped round the diameter of the rail his fingers touched something wet and sticky on the bottom. Likely it had, whatever it was, been there for a while, discovered only now due to the odd angle of Rudd's seated grasp. He wondered what it was, but he didn't pull away though he realized that would be the correct response. It was a mere detail. Gross. Press harder: it oozed from beneath the pads of his fingers.

The brass-colored handrail bracket on the bottom didn't wobble. This was the stairway from the back of Tony's dining room to dry-storage. The paint was cracked and chipped in places. It was splattered with at least three different colors of liquids: grease, tomato sauce, and something yellow. There were more than seven steps; he knew because he and Fenton had made a bet on it some days before. The handrail was walnut stained but almost black in places. There used to be a bare bulb in a ceiling-mounted socket at the bottom of the steps, but now it was a fluorescent ring that was intended as a more economical screw-in replacement for the bulb. The fluorescent ring always took a bit too long to reach its maximum brightness, so the switch was set in the on position by a piece of masking tape, which was pretty much beat to shit because everyone kept trying to turn it off without looking. Writing on the masking tape said *DO NOT TURN OFF;* then in a darker black that must have been added later it demanded *PLEASE!!!* The light was always off now because all the lights were off because the power had gone out six days earlier. Nobody was holding their breath. There were flashlights. There were candles. In the daytime there was sunlight streaming through the cracks in the security shutters as well as through the few bullet holes in the roof.

Miles being shot the day before had something to do with these holes but Rudd hadn't told Langston that part of it, nor had he been asked. It felt like cheating—Langston was blinded early on—but Langston knew he was blind. Rudd wondered if that meant Langston would be spared the visual if not the aural hallucinations of delirium tremens. The two men had discussed it and decided not, after all these were pictures of the mind. Still Rudd wasn't sure. A chance to see again? They were indistinguishable from real sight. Surely Langston, whatever he was now seeing in his mind, wasn't seeing anything like that. Rudd had said to him, "Maybe it'll be a good thing," and then they both had laughed.

So lost in his thoughts was Rudd that the sudden spray of automatic weapon fire against the west side of the building practically startled him off his step. He froze, listened, hoping that someone would handle it. A beat was followed by a second thirty-round clip, and Rudd could almost hear the release and click that filled that beat for the man who held the gun. Rudd didn't know squat about fully automatic weapons or even where one would go to obtain one. He fingered his own Walther PPK/S tucked under his belt and was reassured by his command over it. He'd had this gun for over ten years, one of the German-made models purchased before Interarms acquired the license and began manufacturing them in the United States. That's a fine gun, the Interarms Walther, but Rudd liked owning a German one, something about it, the history yet unaltered. A mouse gun, the other men derided it as, yet Rudd had taken out his share and more thirteen days ago when it counted most.

The shooting was over and still no return fire.

"What the hell's going on!" he yelled, now worried.

In response came the bark of Fenton's Glock twenty-two, forty-caliber for chrissake, all fifteen rounds. Rudd instinctively tapped his own Glock nineteen nine-mm holstered on his ankle. Though a larger and more powerful gun than the Walther, the Glock was carried and considered by Rudd as a backup piece.

"It's about time. We can't have them thinking we're out of ammo, they'll be in here in a second," he added.

"Sorry Rudd. I don't know where Jill is, and Osmond's passed out," explained Fenton from the other room. "I took care of it as soon as I could."

"Yeah. Next time, don't wait for anyone else, just shoot." He waited for a response but none came. Fair enough, Rudd was being a prick and he knew it. Just the beginning, it would get worse for all of them; they would all turn into pricks. Except for Jill maybe, and Osmond since he seemed to be sleeping through his withdrawals. "Say Fenton, come help me take another look at dry-storage after you reload," offered Rudd as a kind of overture.

"Right away, boss."

Smart ass. Burned through his and his sister's inheritance, Rudd had heard of Fenton; but then it was highly probable that Fenton had heard similar things of Rudd. And what the hell did Osmond find enough of to get passed out on? All seemed quiet outside the west wall. Fenton had made the right choice in returning fire with his Glock, perhaps less so in selecting a forty-caliber model. Worst case: Rudd would give his nine-mm to Fenton when the forty-caliber rounds were all gone. Fenton would appreciate that, and he was already familiar with the Glock so it only made sense. Besides, you had to respect a man who carried a plastic gun.

Fenton came fast around the corner and had to pull up short when he saw Rudd still sitting on the top step. He dithered for a moment as if finding it difficult to abandon his plan of bounding down the steps the way he normally would, but he shrugged off the excess energy and sat down next to Rudd, who frankly looked as if he could use a little cheering up.

"Miles is fine," remarked Fenton to break the silence.

"I'd call that a pretty rosy picture," said Rudd.

"I mean the wound, it's nothing. Jill was able to—"

"Spare me the fucking romantic adventures of Nurse Jill and her patients. I've seen quite enough already." Rudd had grown somewhat possessive of Jill, and it ate at him that he could be so easily conquered by this . . . waitress.

"That's neither fair nor kind, Rudd. She's doing what she has to do, just like the rest of us."

Fenton raised his eyes, looking straight at the other man as a way to underscore his defense of the woman. Rudd, though rankled by this declaration of loyalties (suddenly thinking: Jill plus Fenton? Jill plus Fenton?), knew that his friend was right. He decided to leave it alone, and that was something.

"Thanks for covering. You okay on ammo?"

"Box and a half, I'm fine."

"You should say: 'seventy-five rounds,'" but this was given with a smile. Rudd's nature.

Fenton sighed. "Let's call it a box and a half," he said, feeling that it was, after all, getting rather late in the game for this shit.

"Right," said Rudd, rejoined, "right."

"So," said Fenton, "I'm guessing we've got some bad news waiting for us down there." He indicated the steps below them, the dry-storage cellar that lay beyond.

"I'd call that a pretty good guess," said Rudd, and he thought, This is nice, how we can be friends here and make small talk, how no matter how bad it gets Fenton and I can still smile at each other. "I think it's starting to hit me," he added. "I'm getting pricky."

Fenton put his arm around Rudd's shoulder, said, "It's okay, I know, I understand." And he thought, I'm scared, 'cause if Rudd goes down then it'll be me, last, left alone.

The streets outside remained quiet as the two men descended the steps. Of course something must have been happening somewhere in the city, but outside of Tony's, at least for now, it was quiet. Perhaps the distant rumble of a self-serve gas station in flames, its mini-mart long since looted, responding firemen, if any, coming under sporadic fire, kid stuff, perhaps these sounds would reach the ears of someone standing outside of Tony's at that moment. But at that moment no one was.

Dry-storage was a place in which each of the men had spent some time alone, some more than others. The busboy and maybe Jill would have spent time alone there too, but one hardly thought about that as it would have constituted more of a professional obligation than the more spiritual endeavors of the others. Rudd was the last man to be down here alone or so he thought, and what he saw was enough for him to make sure no one ever came down here alone again. But then why would they.

There was a little light down here, but there was also quite a lot to see. Rudd took two flashlights from the first shelf to his left, where they'd always been kept, even before they were needed. He turned to hand one to Fenton only to find him waiting at the foot of the stairs a few steps back.

"What?" Rudd demanded.

"I'm afraid to look. I can smell it from out here; I can't believe we don't smell it upstairs."

"Jesus, Fenton, you are a lightweight. You may recall that our senses may not be operating at peak efficiency. When's the last time you smelled a vodka martini without holding it under your nose? Where you been for the last two weeks?"

"Sixteen days, and pretty close to you is where I've been."

Rudd clicked on his flashlight and turned it on Fenton's face. Fenton glared back, his eyes, Rudd noticed for the first time, as bloodshot as everybody else's.

He turned around the flashlight into his own bloodshot eyes, like a kid playing monster under the sheets. "I know. I'll never forget that. The rest of us, well, we were pretty much stuck with this. But you could've gone another route. We all appreciate how you stood by us."

"Standing. I'm standing by you. And it's mostly you, Rudd. Those other guys aren't anything to me. I'd never even met Miles and Osmond until that first day."

Rudd retraced the few steps to where Fenton stood, handed him the lit flashlight while turning on the one in his other hand. "Give me some moral support here," he said, leading with an arm around Fenton's shoulders, and the two men cast their beams into the once dry storage.

The floor was mostly damp, the bulk of the fluid long gone down the drain that lay in a depressed area in the center of the room. That was perhaps the biggest tragedy, that no one had thought to block that drain, and for an insane moment Rudd wondered if there wouldn't be a way to still chase the liquor lost down it, a siphon, the first few inches.

Crazy. Some small accumulation remained in the form of stray ounces left in the irregular shapes inevitable among so much broken glass. But really, the room was a total loss, almost as if it had been deliberately wrecked bottle by bottle. Yet no one from the outside could have been in here, and no one from the inside could have done this. That was a literal fact: no one inside *could* have done this. Rudd was certain of that, and Rudd was a realist; they all were, men like them everywhere.

No, dry-storage was ruined by the shock absorbed during the previous night's bombings. They all suspected it would be bad, but the shock of the bombings–almost military in their intensity yet obviously nothing more than a highly crafted street offensive–shook the building and likely many buildings for close to a half hour. Plaster crumbled and there were a few minor injuries, but the most terrible part for all of them was the distant sound of breaking glass.

"One of us should have come down–" tried Fenton.

But if he intended to say more Rudd cut him short. "That was my call and now it's made!" he said; then more softly, to himself really: "I thought . . . I mean to say, I kept thinking that it wouldn't be so bad. This late in the game . . . it seems so late, close to the end, I thought maybe better a few less bottles than one less guy." Despondently, he slipped down along the wall until he was sitting in the dampness, which slowly steamed into the backside of his pants. "God, let it be blood," he said, chuckling to himself sadly.

"What was that, Rudd?" asked Fenton gently.

"Oh it's an old joke. A wino falls down in the alley with his last pint in his back pocket. 'God, let it be blood' is what he says when he feels his pocket get wet."

"You did the right thing. I promise. Let's take it from here, okay?" Fenton was scared, but Fenton was also a friend.

Rudd rose back to his full height. "I may have done the right thing," he said, "but that's hardly what was called for."

As one the men shone their flashlights into dry-storage, played the beams across the fallen shelves and cracked and splattered walls so that it briefly became a game of beam chase beam and stopped just short of a giggle or a glance, and the beams were brightest at their centers. This was difficult, this inspection, but it had to be done because it had to be over so the new reality of their situation could begin writing its definition.

"You start on the left," said Fenton, surprising Rudd, not unpleasantly in this time of weakness, by his initiative, "combing your light up and down along the walls. I'll start on the right and we'll pass in the middle for double coverage. Save the floor for last. Forget the ceiling," he added awkwardly. Then after a pause: "If that sounds good to you."

Rudd nodded. "Stop if you see anything, anything at all."

So they began systematically, proceeding just as Fenton had suggested. The shelves in dry-storage were wooden, supported separately at three-foot intervals, short due to the liquid weight they were expected to bear. The shelves were stacked seven high floor to ceiling and held the various bottles three deep—*had* held—the bottles unpacked and kept in stock out of their cases due to Tony's insistence long ago that breakage be done on a bottle-by-bottle basis (now that was funny) during the course of an evening. Hal was a minimalist and liked to keep the bar sparse, only two bottles of well liquor in place and a dedicated bar-back to make sure it stayed that way. Too bad: had the bottles been left in their corrugated cardboard cartons, the way they were in most places, some of them might have survived the drop. But none did. And they all dropped because no shelf, it quickly became apparent, had held; except for the bottom ones, and it was here that Rudd paused his flashlight and said, "Wait a minute!"

Fenton immediately whipped his own beam to the same spot. "What?" he demanded.

"In the back, here." Rudd stepped forward to the shelf, but the crunch of glass under his foot stopped him cold. He turned back to Fenton. "I just thought of something. We may be able to salvage some of these little puddles held in the broken pieces." Fenton nodded and Rudd proceeded more carefully.

He squatted down and reached gingerly behind the second-lowest shelf, which had fallen only in the front so that it hung at something close to a forty-five-degree angle to the wall, crushing the bottles on the front of the lowest shelf, but actually being borne up by some of the bottles at the rear of the lowest shelf. It was these bottles, a precious few of them, that remained unbroken. Rudd extracted a fifth of J&B scotch and held it forth to Fenton as gleefully as any schoolboy showing his mother a gold-starred piece of homework.

"Well done!" cried Fenton.

"You bet your ass!" added Rudd, and they were both momentarily reassured by the sight of a virgin fifth with an unbroken seal.

"Any more? How many?"

And as Rudd handed the bottle to his friend their eyes met over their prize. These were two boys discovering back issues of *Playboy* in a father's closet, though these men had never been boys together.

Rudd probed further with his flashlight then his hand. He pulled out another J&B, held it out for Fenton to take. "Twooo," he said thoughtfully, hopefully, now the accountant. "I think . . . yeah, three."

Now Fenton stood sentry over three full fifths of J&B scotch, which really, for these men at least, was a good thing to have three bottles of. Miles of course would drink anything—for that matter they all would soon enough—but the traditional drink of choice at Tony's was scotch.

"One more, something different," reported Rudd.

It turned out to be a bottle of Malinowa Raspberry Cordial Austrian Liqueur (seventy-six proof). The men stared at the bottle as if it were a copy of *Good Housekeeping* mixed in with the pornography.

"What is it?"

"Seventy-six proof, looks like," answered Rudd as he puzzled over the label. "I don't know what the hell it's doing down here on the scotch shelf."

It seemed they couldn't make up their minds whether to be angry over not finding another bottle of J&B or pleased over finding another bottle of anything, especially something sporting a reasonable proof such as this. There had been something of a liqueur orgy on the seventh day, the stranger stuff being kept to single orders, mostly for the visual appeal of the unusual bottles, and hence not back-stocked down here. They'd burned through it all that night and it wasn't pretty, but it did save them one night's worth of real booze, which now of course was lost.

"I think we should give Osmond his share out of this stuff," said Rudd. "By the way, what the hell is he passed out on?"

"I don't know, but he's out cold in his booth, been that way all morning."

"Son of a bitch. Think he had a bottle hidden?"

"Don't know. Maybe, could've, I suppose."

"Son of a bitch. Well he definitely gets his share from this shit. Passed out. Son of a bitch."

They nodded as one, in evident agreement over the son-of-a-bitchedness of Osmond.

Rudd stood up. "That's it for that shelf," he said.

They silently resumed their scanning, but no other backs of bottom shelves had survived the damage. In less than three minutes they knew and ten minutes after that they admitted: no other unbroken bottles were present in dry-storage. Out of forty-some bottles four had survived. Fenton almost proclaimed this but thought better of it and stopped himself in time, waited.

"That's it," Rudd told him. "Run upstairs and get . . . oh, I don't know, two I suppose, juice containers. We'll pour what we can from these broken bottles into them."

"There are plenty of juice containers. We could have one for scotch and another for vodka, one for whiskey, like that."

"Umm, no. It won't be worth it. We'll end up with five or six almost empty containers: too depressing. Best we just mix it. Believe me, by the time we need it we won't care at all."

Fenton went upstairs, where later he, Rudd, and the others inspected what was salvaged from dry-storage. Balanced on the bar, three fifths of J&B, one of Malinowa Raspberry Cordial Austrian Liqueur (seventy-six proof), one and two-thirds juice containers of Amalgamash, stood the attention of Rudd, Fenton, Miles, Langston, somewhat fortified by the very odor of alcohol, Jill, as sort of a disinterested de facto supervisor or lady principal, and the busboy, who stood passive, cognizant, and secretly resentful of mostly himself. Absent was only Osmond, who remained passed out in his booth and that was frankly just as well because anybody who managed to pass himself out for that long must have had something stashed and though if somebody was gonna do that it would've been Osmond it didn't change the fact that it was wrong at the very least and way outside the conduct agreed upon by this group at the very worst, which it was, the very worst.

One of the juice containers, the one with the lesser volume, was darker than the other. Different colors, even through the translucent plastic, they were, like amber and chestnut.

"How'd that happen?" asked Miles, pointing very closely at but not quite touching the chestnut-colored bottle. This in keeping with the demeanor that prevailed among the men present, one of chemistry students surrounding a rack of fuming test tubes.

And in the role of white-coated professor, Rudd started to answer but was momentarily interrupted by gunfire on the street out front. Everyone paused, as was their custom, bowing their heads as if in prayer. But no one felt threatened, and the attitude of their lips, the way they were mostly, slightly cocked, made the group look like they were merely waiting for someone to finish a coughing fit.

When the shooting stopped, Rudd said, "How's the shoulder, Miles?"

Miles dropped his eyes. "Fine," he muttered, not looking at anybody. "I asked about the bottle."

"Just different puddles as we went along. I don't really see any need to mix it further."

At this Langston fell away from the table in a violent spasm of trembling. "It's okay," he offered, making for his booth. "An early one, it'll pass. But I don't think I should be near the breakables right now."

"Jill, better pour him off a solid double from one of these scotch bottles." He scanned the others for any sign of dissension, knowing that it was unlikely, especially with Osmond not present. "Triage, guys," added Rudd anyway. "We knew it would come to this."

"I'm not the bartender," said Jill right to Rudd, and he thought, you sleep with them and it isn't long before they start giving you this kind of lip.

But he also thought about her breasts. They were on the largish side and Rudd liked that in a woman. He also liked her auburn hair and pert little nose, the way that she gave head and was pretty smart. "Bartender's dead, Jill. He is in the freezer, been there for weeks, but I wouldn't open the door now that the power's out. I was fairly certain that you were aware of this development."

"You can be such an asshole," she said, picking up the scotch bottle, cracking the seal, and pouring off the dosage for Langston.

"I'm a drunk, Jill, it goes with the territory."

Well he's part right, she thought, as she silently crossed the room to Langston's booth. But the territory had more to do with being male than it did with being a drunk. These men, these hopeless desperate men that she was stuck here with, she'd pour their drinks and suck their dicks because as bad as they could be at times they were still better than the men on the outside of that door, because there was a certain nobility in their consistency and pathos, because they'd done what they had to do despite the fact that every one of them was on a greased slide to hell and knew it, and because to leave would be to expose them to a reality that might just break them: she really didn't like them touching her.

"You'll have to hold his head and give it to him," Rudd told her from the bar.

"I know, I know." And she did more or less pour the scotch into Langston's mouth, only missing a drop and that was a good score. The man was trembling but calmed at her touch and again with the liquor. "Not much, I'm afraid," she whispered. "But there isn't much left." That was cold, she thought, and felt bad. This man was really sick. This was serious, like cancer or something. He could die from this.

At the bar Fenton wanted to know, "What did you mean about what was called for?"

"What?" said Rudd.

"Down in dry-storage you said something like, 'I did the right thing but it wasn't called for.' What did you mean by that?"

"I may have done the right thing, but that's hardly what was called for."

"Yeah, right, yeah."

This room was fairly large with a simple slate-topped bar running L on the right side and tables and booths that service the restaurant filling the left side. The bar held a clutch of blond wood stools and it was on two of these that Rudd and Fenton were seated talking, all the remaining liquor in Tony's beheld before them. These two men were members of the Hollydale Country Club and that was how they met. Rudd had been a member longer and met Fenton on the latter's first visit after being invited to join. This fact gave Rudd an edge of seniority that had long since touched all aspects of their acquaintance and friendship. Hollydale was no more–they could guess as much–but they would always be members. They had this over the other men.

The men had been bunking on the black leather benches of the booths and had taken to thinking of them as rooms and being every bit as possessive of them as a bunch of teenage boys. Langston lay in his booth and Jill sat across from him, watching him grope for what little peace could be found in a single swallow of scotch. Before the riots Jill had had little experience with alcohol and way too much experience with sex. By now though she had seen enough evidence in this room to know just how grave the danger was that these men faced. She suspected that they had all hoped to be shot dead before having to face the end of the supply, though Langston, the man quivering on his back before her, was the only one to ever actually confess this to her.

Two stools down from the corner of the bar where Rudd and Fenton sat, that is on the short part of the L and near the door, Miles nursed his shoulder and stared into space. At the far end of the bar from Miles stood the busboy, leaning against the wall. He'd been outside once, days ago, and he was starting to realize that these men would inevitably send him out again. He could, it was true, move around out there, being Latino and thus resembling the average rioter far better than any of the white men of Tony's. No one ever referred to him as anything but busboy; they didn't even know his name and he liked it that way. Only the woman, Jill, once pushed him so hard for a name that he made one up just to get her out of his face. She still whispered it sometimes to him, only when they were alone, as if understanding it was a secret, or perhaps a bond.

Osmond lay face down in his own booth. The most significant fact about Osmond right now was that he was dead, though nobody at Tony's had discovered this yet. He died of alcohol poisoning hours ago. Osmond had always suspected he could pull this off when the time came, and he was right. He had appropriated a fifth of one-hundred-and-fifty-one-proof rum for just this purpose when the end started to feel close. Plan was to simply shoot himself if he failed and remained alive, or vomited, after drinking down the bottle. He did neither. The bottle was now under his chest, incredibly not broken by his enormous girth, his obesity, ironically giving him the appearance of being in mid breath. The others were angry. They knew he had cheated and it pissed them off that he should be sleeping so soundly while someone like Langston who played by the rules was going through hell. They ignored him. Well, that was Osmond.

A good shot normally but no help at all when Langston began screaming so loud and suddenly that Jill started to fly out of the other side of that booth even before a mighty spastic thrust of Langston's chest sent him bolt upright and the table tore up at the bolts as his right shoulder hit it. Everyone froze at the crack of Langston's shoulder as it popped out of its socket. There was a split second before the table teetered to a precarious rest against the bench where a moment ago Jill had been seated. Langston fell to his convulsions, groaning on the loose bolts and crud of the floor of his booth, and everyone knew then that Langston had always been right: he was the first of them to go down.

"DTs comin'!" hollered Miles from his seat at the bar. But his voice held more fear than mockery.

"Shut up, Miles," snapped Rudd anyway. He rose from his seat, grabbing the bottle of J&B from which Langston had just been poured a drink. "Jill! Let's go. I'll hold him down and you get some more of this into him. Try half the bottle—"

He was interrupted by some heavy work on the front door. Not the simple random wall gunfire that they were accustomed to, no this was a very real attempt to enter Tony's. Dents—and some holes—were appearing at an alarming rate on the interior security shutter. No way to tell if there was even anything left of the outside shutter, though Rudd had long since ceased to count on it.

"Fuck!" yelled Miles, whose back was pretty much to and near the shooting. He dove across the bar, western movie style, forgetting about his shoulder until his head-first landing reminded him. "Fuck!" he added through real tears. But this late in the game they had all learned a lot, and it wasn't long before Miles was returning fire from behind the bar.

Langston screamed, thrashed. It was impossible to determine if he knew what was happening. Rudd was close enough to Jill to push her back into Langston's booth. He crouched low and handed her the bottle which he had not for one second forgotten was in his hand.

"Stay down and do what you can for him with this," he told her, for Langston was still the priority; his condition was what they all feared the most, what they would all be most likely to unite against. Rudd took up a position in a forward booth. "Fenton!" he cried over the relentless pounding. "Get that scotch under cover before you do anything else!"

"Is that what's called for, Rudd?" said Fenton, currently too pinned down by his proximity to the door to rise even to a crouch.

Rudd, his Walther locked open just that fast, pulled out his Glock and emptied it at the door. There was a brief lull in the outside fire and Fenton, who like all these men had seen enough to recognize an opportunity, stood straight up and gathered the three remaining glass bottles–two scotch and one liqueur–leaving the less breakable juice containers to stand the next round of fire.

Rudd, reloading, caught sight of him going the long way around the bar. "Good," he said, "don't risk the jump. Put 'em in the sink. Gently–"

Again he was cut short by a spate of shooting, but Fenton had safely made his position behind the bar. He set the bottles in the sink and unholstered his own Glock. Miles was glad for the support on his flank and took the opportunity to snap another clip into his Colt Gold Cup. He turned, nodded at Fenton, slid down a few feet and was able to retrieve the two plastic juice containers from the top of the bar. Jill was doing her best with Langston, who now cognizant of the bottle being placed at his lips was calming somewhat. He made a feeble motion to sit up, but Jill pushed his arm back down and hushed him. The busboy was standing in dry-storage, not so much afraid as uninvolved. No one had heard from either of Osmond's two forty-four-magnum Smith & Wesson model twenty-nines, though the shooting showed no sign of letting up.

"*Some*body's knockin'!" screamed Langston from the floor of his booth, using a southern drawl, which nobody present had ever heard him use before.

The shooting stopped, as if just as surprised as the rest of them at this half-assed speaking in tongues.

"Hah!" yelled Langston, claiming credit of sorts but more likely too delirious to know or care.

It only seemed to precipitate more shooting, and perhaps it really did. More than anything it broke Rudd–temporarily, it had happened before when things went spinning far beyond his control–broke his temper.

"Jill! You either shut him the fuck up or I'll put a round in him myself!" With that Rudd, in disregard of the continuing gunfire, stood like some driven demigod, a Patton or a Robert Duvall, a pop-culture icon impervious to harm but one whose legend would never leave this room. He walked so straight and sure to the booths that Jill covered the oblivious Langston with her own body, fearing for a moment that he might have meant it, might now be on his way to shoot this man, her charge, through the head.

But Rudd only walked by, a strained "I mean it" issuing like steam from between his clenched teeth. "Osmond!" he bellowed. And again upon arriving at that man's booth, his still inert body so drunk, so very passed out, "Osmond!" A bullet pierced Rudd's thigh, clean through the flesh, harmlessly if such an occurrence can be described in such a manner. Nobody noticed, not even Rudd, so intent was he on righting this wrong, on awaking the passed-out-on-a-cheat Osmond and bringing him to this battle. Not that its course would have been altered by Osmond, but the fearsome bark of his twin forty-fours would have been a welcome voice in its sporadic refrain.

Even as he approached the booth and squatted with his left hand contacting his own fresh wound Rudd failed to notice either pain or blood. Not until he placed his hand, now covered in his own blood, on Osmond's back, shaking him violently in an effort to revive him, did Rudd see the blood. And because what he saw first was blood on Osmond he assumed then that the blood on him came from Osmond and this was his first, both true and false, sign that something was wrong with this large man beyond being dead drunk.

Rudd stared at his hand. He stared at the blood on Osmond's back. He even stared at his thigh, saw the wound or at least the hole in his pants, and thought for a perverse moment that if he was destined to stain his pants with Osmond's blood then wasn't it propitious to have done so in the same spot where they'd been torn anyway.

Then Jill was behind him. Langston had fallen silent and there was a lull in the shooting. In fact the shooting had stopped, Jill was sure of it. "You're hurt," she said to Rudd.

"No, it's Osmond," Rudd said, placing his hand on the man again and shaking gently. "I think he's dead."

With that they heard a muffled crunch as the bottle Osmond had drunk himself to death with and was lying on finally gave way to Rudd's gentle nudging. The dead man's huge chest lowered a bit, as if in final exhale.

A single gunshot cracked from the front of Tony's. Outside. After the Hollywood ping of a ricochet they all heard the shattering collapse of one of the two bottles of J&B that Fenton had placed in the sink behind the bar.

"Well that sure didn't sound like Malinowa Raspberry Cordial Austrian Liqueur!" lilted Langston, and then he began snoring.

Day 1

R udd sauntered into Tony's at about 3:30 P.M. He hoped
that nobody would notice he was wearing a backup; then
he hoped that somebody might. Maybe that waitress, Jill was
her name. After all, most women, despite what they said,
viewed a gun like a dick only better. Point was that it wouldn't
do for Rudd, the great believer, proponent, and prophet of
enduring Civil Obedience to be perceived as paying any attention to scattered media reports of a small situation—which was
probably well in hand by now anyway—brewing at an obscure
intersection in some godforsaken minority section of the city.
Best just put a torch to the whole block and be done with it,
and in fact that's exactly what Rudd knew would happen before
it was allowed to get out of hand.

All the same there had been other little problems in other
little cities over the last few years and some of those had
become big problems requiring bigger problem solvers and
inconveniencing the community-at-large for a day or two.
Lessons had been learned, to be sure. Still, it smelled like a
two-gun day, and most men he knew routinely carried backups
every day. Likely nobody'd even heard anything; it was a minor
joke at the club an hour ago between him and Fenton.

That was his last drink, and Rudd could feel it was long past time for his next. He'd invited Fenton, who had never been to Tony's, ostensibly to meet a few of the guys, none of whom Rudd much cared for, but really to impress him with the caliber of bar he was a regular in. They were coming in separate cars, Fenton wanting to squeeze in nine holes and Rudd wanting to get a discreet start on the evening's drinking so that when his friend walked in he could say of his fourth scotch something like: What timing! I was just about to order a second.

Tony's was as usual for this hour on whatever day it was. There was Miles, shitfaced, catching Rudd's eye. "Hey!" he said, "Heard about the riot?"

A man named Osmond, corpulent and known only modestly to Rudd, took the opportunity to shoot him a nonetheless familiar glance somehow apropos of Miles's remark. Rudd took a stool on the corner of the L, between the two men. There was no one else seated at the bar.

The bartender, standing near but not chatting with Jill, the waitress and only woman in Tony's at that moment, strode from the far end of the bar and spun a napkin into place. "How are you, Rudd," he said, extending his hand, rhetorically.

"Jesse James," said Rudd, though this man's name was neither. He liked this trick for certain types, bartender types and mailman types, whose names he knew but felt inexplicably uncomfortable using. Rudd felt that calling these people something absurd would make it seem as if he were beyond the point of mere familiarity with them while keeping his hands clean at the same time. Everything I say sounds stupid, he thought very deeply and privately as he silently half-pointed in the direction of the J&B. His way of asking for the usual.

But the bartender was already on it. "Me too," said Osmond, who always drank vodka martinis as far as Rudd could tell. Miles preferred Cutty Sark scotch but usually drank something silly. Today his drink was up and black as coal.

"You and your riots," said Rudd derisively but with a smile. The bartender, exceedingly quick as ever, had the two drinks ready and dropped them into place, Osmond's first after picking up his empty with the same hand. Okay, thought Rudd, he *was* closer.

"It's all he can talk about," said Osmond. "All afternoon." He belched matter-of-factly.

"What was that?" Miles wanted to know. "I bet you think it's okay to burp as long as you're drinking vodka martinis." But then he belched himself. Of these three men Miles and Osmond had known each other the longest.

It suddenly occurred to Rudd that Miles belonged in a sixties Jack Lemmon movie; then it sadly occurred to him that they all did. He downed his drink in one gulp. He hated that thought. Riot my ass, was a better way to think. Small magic with a dash of eye contact brought Rudd another drink.

He touched the glass as the alcohol from the first began to tickle him and it felt well to be in this place. Very familiar, even Miles and Osmond a comfort, the cool of the emptiness, between the rushes, the staff would call it. But then the only staff present was Jill and the bartender. Rudd assumed there had to be kitchen staff somewhere in the back, prep cooks and such, but other than the occasional white-aproned brown-faced illegal alien timidly slipping out for a coke for the cook looking like some beaten-down shifty Toby thinking *Kunta Kinte, Kunta Kinte,* these people remained transparent to the clientele. Just as well. This day was tense and getting tenser, though Rudd could barely admit this to himself, and the clean room sparsely dotted with only white faces was something of a comfort. Very familiar, very predictable, the best single reason to keep coming back.

"Say, Rudd," began Osmond, "you don't think this is going anywhere, do you, this bullshit across town?" He sounded frightened, this big man, unless Rudd was projecting his own secret concerns; oddly, it endeared him to Rudd.

" 'Course not," he replied.

"I know, I know." He laughed but it came out as a snort just short of embarrassing due to his bulk. "I'm just hoping you can calm down this excitable asshole. It's all he can talk about. All afternoon." He indicated Miles with the base of his martini glass as he lifted it to bury his face.

"Fuck if I'm worried," said Miles. He patted the space under his left arm, under his jacket. "I'm covered, as usual."

"Still carrying around that antique?" Rudd couldn't resist any more than Miles could resist showing off his Colt at every opportunity.

"Yeah, well I'm still saving up for one of those nice new plastic guns like the one you got strapped around your ankle right now." He gave Rudd a look like, I got ya', and the other man tensed, wanting badly but not daring to look at his ankle right now and see for himself exactly what was visible. Miles continued, "Besides what are you talking antiques with that German piece of shit you carry every day."

So he let it go and maybe I'm not all that busted, thought Rudd. Try: "Truth be told my Walther *has* been jamming lately. That's why I've taken to the Glock most every day too." He gave his firmest most authoritative nod— one jerk—thinking: You're nothing to me, you're nothing to me.

"Right," said Miles, doing a better job than usual of masking his true thoughts, if he had any. "Say Ossie, show him your cannons." To Rudd: "You're not gonna believe this. He carries these fuckers wherever he goes, long as I've known him."

A big grin swept over Osmond's face as, looking down the bar to confirm they weren't being watched, he unbuttoned his jacket and turned to Rudd.

"Jesus," said Rudd, duly impressed. "Forty-four mags? Smiths?"

Osmond, already nodding quickly and still grinning, squealed, "Twin model twenty-nines!" He raised his eyebrows as if to underscore the exhibition he was granting before buttoning his jacket quickly. Then he quickly stiffened, turned to his drink, and affected a posture of nothing-funny-goin'-on-here.

Rudd marveled at the man, wanted to look around for the teacher. Well, he supposed, if I was that fat I could play double Dirty Harry too. "Well I suppose Tony's is safe," he quipped and immediately regretted it when he saw the jolt of fear pass through Osmond. This guy really *was* worried.

Miles, either oblivious, uncaring, or more skillful than Rudd, pitched in with, "Oh, Tony's is safe all right. Anybody that could afford to be in here has too much to lose to ever let anybody else walk in. Besides, didn't this place used to be a police station or something? I mean, it's built like a fortress. You ever drive by here at four in the morning and see those security shutters? It's like a fucking bank vault! Tony must be one paranoid fuck." He polished off his disgusting drink and hollered at the bartender, who was ready for anything from Miles, "Let's try a Pernod rocks with a splash—just a splash—of Evian."

Jesus, thought Rudd. "Savings and loan," he said. "Some screwball tried to build it bulletproof but got indicted before he could open. Guy named Farrell, I think, built funds out of a mini-mall branch and meant for this to be a more seemly location. Feds never moved in and Tony got it for a song, remodeled. Double shutters, by the way, inner and outer." This last he said directly to Osmond, like: See, you want information, you come to me.

It was true; Tony's was a patently defensible place, though no one had ever given it much thought until today. Maybe a joke now and again, a drunken remark or a jab at the drink prices being higher than even Hollydale. Not that Miles or Osmond would know that. It was one thing to be able to afford to be a regular at Tony's, quite another to be a member of Hollydale. Rudd glanced out the window by way of following his over-the-shoulder gesture toward the security shutters and happened to see Fenton's cream-colored Lexus making a U-turn in pursuit of a parking place. No valets at this hour. No cops with the time to bust you for a U-turn at this moment. C'mon, lighten up.

Miles, inspecting his Pernod as if it were an Erlenmeyer flask, taunted, "You been researching this, Rudd? That why you're here on such a *volatile* afternoon?"

But Rudd barely heard him, or didn't want to. Enough was enough, and now that Fenton was about to walk through the door Rudd wanted to suspend the conversation, such as it was, rather than waste a possible witty retort (something might come up) without his friend here to witness it. Not now, not when he was so close. Might be something good, really good, something worth repeating at the club tomorrow. Fenton would cajole him to repeat it and Rudd could demur until whomever they were with joined the course and he finally, coyly, condescended. "I'm here every day," he said, and once again he regretted speaking too soon, for this sounded too defensive.

He swiveled his stool fully toward the door, preemptively, placing his elbows on the bar behind him.

Fenton walked in. "Found it!" he announced, rather blithely Rudd thought, and it occurred to Rudd that Fenton probably believed everything he told him.

"I had no doubt," he said, brightening immediately, infected with his own optimism like catching back your own cold. These clods at the bar really had him going. "Grab a stool. We're comparing penis size." Something Fenton would say, so naturally Rudd had picked up the habit of saying such things to Fenton, or even just around him.

Fenton was well aware of the dynamic of their relationship, and he was sensitive to it. Though there were seats available on either side of Rudd, he elected to sit on the far side of the large man to Rudd's left. This would more effectively distribute the conversational group. For no reason he thought of silverware, napkins, his sister's wedding, and buying a second tuxedo. "Hi, I'm Fenton," he said, extending his hand to the large man.

"Give me a damn second for chrissake," Rudd jumped in. "Fenton, Osmond," finger, tocking, this man, that man. "Miles," he added via thumb over shoulder. "What are ya' drinking, Fenton?"

The bartender, already there, looked at Rudd with a jackass smile. Rudd always tipped well, and the bartender wanted to say something familiar and facetious like, You want to come back here and pour it too? but fuck it, he thought.

Rudd drained his drink. Remembering, he said, "I was just about to order—" He had to let it go; he couldn't very well yell a lie across the room. He had expected Fenton to sit next to him; then he could have muttered quick and low, a second.

"We got anything but Colt 45 malt liquor," Miles put in. "You gotta loot a liquor store if you want that."

"Perrier's fine to start," Fenton said more to Miles than the bartender, spotting right away that the latter was enough of a pro to respond to light neglect, to take it as a code for a nice tip in exchange for straight service, and that the former, likewise, would respond to a lick of attention, sycophancy even. "A topical reference, I take it," he added, surprising Rudd, then, going to bat for same: "You don't look like a slave to the media, Miles."

At this Osmond opened his jacket to Fenton, perhaps taking advantage of the bartender's turned back. "Twin forty-four mags," he said, snapping it shut.

"Not only the biggest penis, but two of them," said Rudd.

"Colt forty-five, as a matter a fact," said Miles over raised forefinger in response to Fenton's inquisitively raised eyebrows. "Gold Cup. And yourself?"

"Glock twenty-two," said Fenton without hesitation. "Forty-caliber."

Miles exhaled in a vaguely derisive fashion, too fast and too hard, prompting Rudd to say to Fenton, "Miles is less than awed by our plastic guns, as he calls them."

"Let's hope he doesn't end up getting shot by one," said Fenton with a smile.

"But then you'd be aiming at the wrong color," said Miles. "I like your friend, Rudd. Too bad he doesn't drink."

Rudd watched Fenton let this slip, as he knew he would. Fenton was a bit of a bleeding heart, Rudd knew, but also smart enough to not let it interfere with anybody's drinking. That shit was better left in the miserable little dive bars that dotted downtown, places like Dewey's Lucky Shot, where Rudd once happened to witness a fight many years ago. About what he didn't know, could've been racial, plenty of poor blacks and Latinos glaring at each other over their draft beers in that place. Those guys always seemed to have knife scars. Rudd patted his Walther. "He drinks," he said. "He's just not a drunk like us." This, the men's favorite form of self-deprecation, brought them all back to good humor.

And it was with laughter running about their faces that they all noticed, almost as one, the busboy, straining against his white shirt and tie, carry Tony's old nineteen-inch RCA television out to its occasional, Super Bowl–type resting place on the flat area above and behind the liquor bottles on the back of the bar.

"You're fucking kidding me," whined Rudd as the kid plugged in the set.

"Big news day," said the bartender, turning it on.

"What the hell does that mean?" demanded Osmond. " 'Big new day'?"

"*News*, not *new*," said Miles, strikingly annoyed, eyes glued to the broadcast now shaping up with the swiftness of solid-state.

"What do you say to that, Rudd?" said Osmond, trying hard to laugh but clearly in need of a little reassurance.

Rudd noticed the busboy staring right at him, rather brazenly, he thought, from the back of the room. The kid disappeared behind the corner. "These local guys are so afraid of being scooped that they'd cover the mayor's morning fart if they could get in his bathroom."

Everybody laughed, and Rudd regretted he hadn't been funnier.

Shot here was from SkyCam3, hovering over the action, presumably where it had begun, though it seemed to have spread as far as the video could see. Rudd saw the busboy again, this time watching not him but the television from around the corner. The aerial shot took in the river, which seemed to be providing a border of sorts to the activity though small plumes of smoke could be seen rising from scattered areas on the other side, even from the historical district, which Rudd thought was pretty fucked, it being their history as much as his (not that he'd want to have to make that argument to Fenton). Rudd wondered if this would be happening in winter. Fires in snow, harder to start but harder to put out as well. So it is a riot, he thought. Then he realized what he'd just thought, and he thought it again to be sure, to get a real good taste. So it *is* a riot. RYE-OTT.

Nobody was laughing now. They were silently watching a remote unit capturing live video of a firefighter being shot in the back as he ascended a ladder. His yellow-slickered body tumbled down and the video went dead. Unit chasing ass out of there, Rudd imagined. "Jesus," he said, and the silence was broken.

Miles turned to Rudd with an I-told-you-so expression, and the latter waited to see if this guy was enough of a jerk to follow through. Neither of them was ever to know, for at that moment Langston, another regular, pushed through the door, carrying with him a breeze that overturned the top two or three napkins from a stack on the corner of the bar.

Langston, a tall man with red hair, stood at the door and looked earnestly at the men, eyes pausing only a moment on Fenton, whom he likely was able to deduce the identity of. He opened his jacket and revealed his Beretta 92F for the whole bar to see. Then he looked directly at Rudd. "There's a crowd formed on the corner of Whitewood and Palmer, not a mile from here," he said. "Some son of a bitch tossed a brick through my windshield and I had to plow right through them. I might have hit somebody; I don't know for sure, but I almost hope so. I don't know what would have happened if I'd had the top down. No bullshit now. The day is upon us."

At this Osmond, gagging and heaving, bolted from his stool to the restroom. Langston's eye followed him for a second but returned quickly to Fenton.

"Fenton?" he asked, crisply, militarily.

"That's right," asserted Rudd, standing. This was going to be his show—he could feel that now—and it would go easier all around if that were made clear right from the start. "This is Langston," he said to his friend. "I've told him as much about you as I have you about him. Have a seat, Langston." He snapped back down on his stool without any further look at Langston, who did indeed sit down, on his left in fact.

"Drink!" barked Langston at the bartender.

The bartender paused a beat, wrapped up in the television as he was and beginning to wonder whether fetching a Glenlivet for Langston was the best use of his time right now, in light of the events unfolding on screen and, evidently, in street. But he got the drink. Brought the bottle, too, set it on the bar next to Langston's drink. *The Glenlivet*, it said on the label, *unblended—twelve years old*.

"What the heck is this for," said Langston though he already knew the answer.

"Whitewood and Palmer?" said Rudd.

"We were just there," said Fenton.

"Well?" demanded Langston anyway. He looked up, chase, try to meet the eyes, that bartender.

They all looked at the bartender. A circle of red, formed on his chest, was growing in the white cotton of his shirt. They saw it, then they remembered hearing the sharp crack—not a shatter, more a click—of a pane of glass being pierced. The bartender's knees folded, and he crumpled dead to the floor.

Jill screamed for the first and last time of her adult life. It was the next sound to follow the glass, or would be in the record of Rudd's memory. He looked at her. She was looking at him and she stopped as if embarrassed, which she wasn't. "Back here," she said to him.

To him she said it, and for that reason he never thought about not going to her. He left his stool, passed Langston and Fenton, both already risen and on their way around the bar to assist the bartender though everybody knew beyond doubt that he was dead, like the riot had supercharged things, turning the very air into a medium of communication. He noticed Osmond, frozen, staring from the corridor that led to the restrooms. Rudd wanted to slap him into some kind of activity, and he wondered at the sudden proliferation of such thoughts in his head, when and why exactly it began. It *had* begun, not long ago but it had. There was a duty here. Impossible to perceive the world except through one's own senses. Make your best guess. Day of instinct, higher motivations maybe. Osmond was Osmond. Osmond was not Rudd. That later. Now Jill.

"Here," she said when he approached her.

She led him around the corner, back to where the kitchen lay. As far as Rudd could tell there was only one person there, a young black with two enormous cans cradled in his arm. He was reaching into the freezer, working a way to carry a box of beef without dropping the cans. Just as he managed it he caught sight of Rudd and Jill and immediately fled out the open back door. This prompted Rudd to notice how bare the place looked—though he'd never been here before. Things were missing, knives, pots, food, as well as the staff. Rudd heard a gunshot in the distance beyond the open door.

"Close that," he said to Jill. "Lock it."

He walked quickly across the room, throwing open doors, inspecting closets and nooks, small rooms beyond the kitchen where the business of the restaurant was conducted. What he was looking for was, well, the enemy, though this word had not yet presented itself in his mind. He was merely looking, urgently. He knew he had to, that it was the appropriate thing to do. When he was finished and had confirmed the place empty he returned to Jill, now standing where they had entered the room. The back door, he noticed, was not only closed and locked but the three large horizontal bars that made it virtually impenetrable had been dropped into place.

"What's that for?" Jill asked him, indicating his hand.

He followed her eyes. He was holding his Walther, and when he saw it he remembered drawing it, but when he drew it, during his check of the back, he didn't realize what he was doing. Again, the right move, but would these people have been armed? Would he have shot somebody, say some dish-washer cowering behind the sink with a chef's knife? Would anybody who felt the need to hide really be so dangerous, so much of a threat?

"Door was open," he said simple and plain. "Anybody could have gotten in." But he was ready for another drink, and given that, he would be ready for anything. He put the gun away. "Up front," he said.

When they returned to the bar they found the men back on their stools. The bartender, now covered with a table-cloth, lay where he fell with one foot peeking from under the white. Jill peeled away from Rudd, sat at a table, and began folding napkins. This was the situation. Napkins should be folded, Rudd guessed. He thought about helping her as a way to comfort her, but she seemed okay and the men needed him too and he needed a drink. Without thinking too much about it he took the same stool he had been sitting on before, as if the others had been saving it for him. There were bottles on the bar—someone had even thought to put up a fifth of J&B, probably Fenton—but otherwise it felt so natural that Rudd had to glance down at the tablecloth to confirm the nightmare. The exposed shoe confirmed it. Sporadic gunfire continued outside in the not-so-distance.

He filled his glass from the bottle of J&B. Right away it warmed him, too fast to be trusted but he was grateful nonetheless. Fenton, he noticed, was drinking too. No bottle but his drink was the same color as Rudd's. That would explain the J&B bottle; still, he had moved it in front of Rudd's stool when he was done. A modicum of loyalty, more in the choice of drink itself, that a victory of sorts.

"Like that scotch?" Rudd wanted to know.

"It's working," said Fenton.

"It always does," Rudd told him, now feeling damn near drunk, what with this drink and all he had earlier. "Hell of a thing," he added, "you starting to drink five minutes after our only bartender gets shot." Miles's shoulders began to rise and fall. At first in his peripheral vision Rudd thought he was crying, but by the time he turned to look Miles had progressed from giggle to guffaw. Osmond took the cue. They all laughed. They laughed hard and they drank and they filled their glasses and laughed some more. Jill folded napkins.

Day 2

Rudd awoke smiling, still drunk from the late night before. The smell of coffee hung about the room. As always it struck him as some impossible ideal, that coffee smell, some go-getter bullshit that only served to remind him of how important it was to get a Bloody Mary into him ASAP. Outside a lone gunshot came muffled to his ears, and he remembered how he and Langston had gotten drunk enough to go outside in the middle of the night and secure the external security shutters. It had been relatively quiet and was as good a time as any, but when they got outside the sky glowed orange over the burning city and the crackle of flames carried hoots and hollers down and up the streets and blocks. Once the shutters were locked they had to walk around long to the rear door. Rudd had provided cover while Langston dipped into his car for his pocket cellular phone and several boxes of nine-mm hollow points he always kept under the seat; then they scurried back into Tony's like kids playing fort, walkie-talkies. Big deal: Langston never got much of a signal inside Tony's which is why he left the phone in his glove compartment in the first place. Besides, Tony's phone still worked and the network was now completely down to boot.

Rudd lifted his head. He had passed out on one of the benches up front where waiting-list diners waited for their tables. He was the first one up—second: Jill stood behind the coffee warmer at the far end of the bar, glaring at him as if daring him not to make a dent in the still-full pot.

"What are you going to do about him?" she demanded, pointing at the bartender.

Bartender, he thought. His smile deepened that she had put this in his lap, assumed it was his problem, his decision, his charge. What are *you* going to do. "Put him out the back door, I guess," he said.

"You can't do that. I've been awake for hours and they're out there. I've been hearing noises all night. I think some bullets even hit the door. We can't open that door anymore. Please." She bit her lip, then poured a cup of coffee for him without asking, added cream roughly but no sugar. A guess and it was right. "Besides, I don't want him out there."

So he'd have some coffee, if for no other reason than to calm her down. "The freezer," he asked. Said.

"Good idea," she said, walking across the room with his coffee.

He felt taken. "I'll need some Irish whiskey for that."

She stopped short, put the coffee down on the bar abruptly, and walked back around for the bottle. Evidently she'd stepped through this response already, something to think about during the deep and scary night. He felt chastised but amused nonetheless. This was so typical, one of several tacks they take when faced with an indefatigable drunk.

"Pour it yourself," she said, setting the bottle down next to his coffee but not moving, just standing there behind the bar.

Not far from the stiff, he thought. Nineteen seventies TV bad guy talk. So she couldn't go through with it. Well, it was a start. He sat up, grunting inadvertently.

"Oh here."

He watched her splash some whiskey into the mug, too much as a better choice than being accused of adding too little. She walked back around. That wasn't hard, he thought, but he knew she probably was looking for a way to distance herself from El Stiffo. Rudd laughed and some snot came out of his nose and that was unacceptable. Time to clean up the act, have some coffee.

"Coffee. My dad drank coffee," he told her when she handed him the mug. Drink it down now, boy. That's hot. Best drink it down. Hurt. No hurt. Not Jill hurt. Drink it down, boy. White boy drinkin' down his coffee. Truck stop boy drinkin' down his joe. Rudd was eleven when he saw a man in the men's room (of a truck stop) pee from five—call it six—feet away from the urinal and make it. Call *that* an education. Thing to do now is put the stiff in the freezer.

"We'll drag him in as soon as some of the guys get up. I'll get Fenton to give me a hand."

"Fenton. That the guy you brought in yesterday? You seem pretty chummy; how come you don't bring him in more often?"

Conversational stuff now, distraction. "Actually yesterday was the first time." He lifted his head to confirm that they were out of earshot from the other men. "Some of these guys, they're fine to drink with, but not quite the class of men that Fenton normally associates with." Maybe not so conversational.

"But you are."

"Yeah." Dammit. Yeah.

"But Langston's not."

Rudd stood up, with difficulty yet unwilling to give that away. Not that he was fooling anybody, he knew from experience, and experience was something that this woman Jill evidently had her share of. "I get my own whiskey for now. You can answer your own questions."

She saw that she had offended him and regretted it. She needed him; her instincts told her, he was her best shot at getting out of Tony's alive, getting to somewhere safe— though where that might be she'd have a hard time saying. The television was painting a pretty gloomy picture. Yet there were still cities in which the violence had been kept to a minimum. It would still be at the spreading stage this early on. Certainly a slowing stage would follow, a time for people to catch their breath and realize exactly what they were doing to each other. But there were no guarantees, not even among the men in here, and this Rudd, Jill knew, would be the one to be next to if things really fell apart. He wasn't there yet. He was a long way from it. But like herself, he would be able to do what had to be done. She merely had to place herself in that category, something that he would find had to be done.

He nudged himself onto a stool, her watching and him knowing she watched, in front of the bottle, where she had left it and him moving clumsily, backward and confused yet getting the point across with the overkill effort of one who moves to make a point overkilledly. Yet she also noted a basic grace to the action, a practice. One of the men— Jill didn't know who—issued a single snore from the booths, and it served to make her realize how quiet things had become outside. She thought about a shower, worried that she smelled, inanely wondered if her bra was dirty. Should have worn a black one. Of course they show through a white shirt, and how was she to know she'd be stuck here for who knows how long without a shower. Something she'd heard as a little girl about men hating dirty bras. Those dirty white training bras and her mom getting on her about something no doubt unrelated like keeping her room clean, getting on her with some stupid unrelated offhand remark and her now twenty-seven. Dirty white bra, have to wash it sooner or later with something from the cleaning supply closet, napkin service no doubt having been canceled with yesterday's firemen murders.

Rudd heard that snore. He thought about how he was being a jerk and how quiet it was outside and how—as much as he'd like to sit here and drink all day—this woman was depending on him to move the bartender's body into the freezer. He wanted to turn and look at her, make nice and steal another glance at what must be magnificent breasts and at the very least exactly the size he preferred. But he wasn't being depended on to think about breasts anymore than he was being depended on to drink. He looked at his Rolex; that snore occurred at 10:17 A.M.

Downing his coffee, he stood. Jill was watching him, but rather than say something he merely snapped his countenance to determination and spun about to carpe the fucking diem, acting having the earmarks of being a sounder bet. The dark restaurant lay before him like a mausoleum. Men strewn about, place sealed shut. Creepy.

"Why's it so dark in here?" he asked her, turning back around and taking a half step.

"The shutters are down. A little light gets in through the cracks, but not much."

"Jill, I know. What I'm asking is why the lights are off."

"I didn't want to wake everybody up."

"Well I do. Why don't you show me where all the switches are." That went well, he thought.

She nodded, evidently pleased with the request, and walked past his follow. As they walked he caught a glimpse of Langston tucked away in one of the booths. He remembered being in Rome as a kid, on a tour of the Catacombs. All those corridors and coves, bare light bulbs suspended from the ceiling. He had thought, Okay, if I get lost down here the thing to do is start breaking light bulbs and follow the remaining light out to the exit. He had thought that was a pretty clever plan at the time. Later he realized how fucked he'd be with that plan if he ended up in a dead end, dark and alone. And clever.

"Wake up, Langston!" he shouted, startling Jill but eliciting no apparent response from the intended victim. They both stared at the sleeping man for a moment. "Lights," he said to her. "Wait a second. Where's the TV?"

"The busboy took it back to the kitchen early this morning. He's watching it there."

"Yeah, well he can bring it back up here and watch it with the rest of us."

"I think he was only trying to be considerate of the ward."

The ward. Funny, thought Rudd, it's really funny. Sarcasm, yet she doesn't seem to be a drinker. "A Latino kid carrying off a television set: probably the same scene that was on it when he unplugged it. Don't trust him too far," he whispered.

Jill was saved from having to respond to this by their arrival at the first panel of lights. She rattled them off: bar, booths, front, painting illumination. She pointed to another panel ten feet away near the corridor to the restrooms: back hall, those two tall lamps. He waited until she was through then used the full of his hand to slide all switches to their brightest positions, walked to the other panel and did the same. A chorus of groans arose from the room. Rudd ignored them.

"There's more in the kitchen," she told him, and they went straightaway.

Sure enough there was the busboy, leaning back on a chair with his feet up on a sink, watching the televised riot coverage while using a wooden cooking spoon to munch from an enormous can of beans.

Rudd felt the rage of his residual drunk seize him. "Hey, Paco!" he yelled, slapping the boy's legs from the sink. "You speak English?" To Jill: "He speak English?"

"His name's not Paco," she said coldly.

The busboy set down his beans and rose to a standing position, aggressively taking a step toward Rudd.

"I don't care what his fucking name is," said Rudd as he opened his jacket to expose the Walther. All the time he watched the kid's eyes, enjoying the reaction there but not finding it as satisfying as he had hoped. "Sit down," he said. "We've got to go over the rules."

"I can do rules," he spit back, leaning against the sink, and Rudd, Jill, and most of all the busboy knew that he had won the round.

"Fine." He took a position against a stove opposite the busboy. "Get me some more coffee, Jill." Then looking at her: "Half coffee, half whiskey." Back to the busboy: "My Hispanic brother and I need to have a chat."

"You don't even know what race I am," said the kid derisively after Jill had left the room.

"Sure I do. Not white. Now let's get down to business."

The busboy listened though he could have guessed most of what he heard. First he was told that if he was planning to leave he should leave now. As Rudd was explaining the importance of him declaring his loyalties the busboy was thinking how mad he was at himself for losing his temper earlier, for falling out of character in front of this white man, now babbling about being able to provide protection. Food would be inventoried and rationed. More detailed plans regarding the food would be developed soon. The busboy was not to drink any of the liquor. The television stayed in the front room at all times. The woman brought the coffee in and handed it to the man. Rudd was in charge, but the busboy should be prepared to do whatever was asked of him because they were all in this together. Rudd and the other men would be happy to pay him for his time here if he chose to stay. At this he almost laughed as he had already hidden the lunch receipts in a safe place. Rudd babbled on. The busboy knew he couldn't get back to his neighborhood now, not after the things he'd seen on the TV last night. The riot would end in a few days, and he'd be in much better shape if he were discovered by the National Guard in the company of these white men. Rudd was sorry about the Paco thing. When he finally got home he could always claim they'd made him stay. He'd have the bag from yesterday's lunch plus whatever money these guys gave him to show his people about his loyalties. The man, Rudd, drained his coffee mug and said something about being glad they'd reached an understanding. The busboy thought they'd always had one.

By the time Rudd returned to the front room everyone was awake except Osmond and pretty much gathered at the back end of the bar, clustered near the coffee pots. Jill was a natural den mother, which was probably for the best, and Osmond's steady snoring rang not so much in protest of the morning as refusal to be excluded from the conversation. Desultory gunfire pierced the morning outside as if so many lawnmower jockeys and leaf-blower-wielding immigrants had merely exchanged their noisemakers. The busboy came in carrying the television back to what would become its permanent location, and though Rudd hoped for the kid's sake he wouldn't be looking *too* sheepish in front of everybody, he was nonetheless angered when their eyes locked and the kid's expression was one of utter detachment, if one were to give him the benefit of the doubt that is.

"So how do you like Tony's?" said Rudd, sidling up to and putting his arm around Fenton. Clubstyle. Boys at Hollydale. . . . Maybe not here and now, he thought, dropping his arm.

Fenton smiled politely at the sarcasm. Rudd took the snub in stride, learning to be a good leader. People had homes, he supposed, other places to be, like Hollydale maybe. He looked around the room; he couldn't think of any place he'd rather be.

"Thanks for the wake up, Rudd." This from Langston, at Rudd's left.

"Well, dammit, I'm sorry, but—"

The tall man turned on him, silencing him with a subtle facial tick that would have looked affected on anybody else, maybe just anybody without red hair. "No, I mean it. Here you are taking care of business while we're all sawing wood. Won't do, and I'm ashamed. Don't normally sleep past eight." He put his hand on Rudd's arm. "I won't again. You can count on me."

Rudd caught himself short. About face. "I appreciate that, Langston," he said simply and not without some dignity.

But Langston was looking at the television; they all were. The busboy had managed to turn it on and somehow vanish without Rudd noticing. Probably back to his can of beans, but big deal: beans is something we can spare.

"My God!" said Osmond, eyes glued on the screen as he staggered drunken from his booth like some retarded giant.

No one else could speak. What was on the screen looked more like a tiny Tokyo being trampled in a sixties Japanese monster movie than anything else in their experience. It was like a hallucination for these men: you know it's not really there so you try to think your way around it. Only this was working in reverse: they knew it really was there yet they were unable to convince their senses that what they were seeing was real. The helicopter would record the undoing of twentieth-century America. Right now the skyline of the city—unclear exactly how *live* the shot was, but it was daylight—was aflame. Not a single high-rise bore no smoke or flame. Portions of some of the buildings were actually missing, presumably from internal explosions unless some National Guard artillery had been badly mishandled. There was no clear battle line, at least not from this shot, and how could there be; this was happening inside, from everywhere: blood oozing up through a submerged strainer. You're the good guy. You're the stainless-steel wire.

Moving in now, this intrepid news crew, for a closer look at some fallen comrades. Some panicky audio soon cut out as they approached the wreckage of NewsBird 9, shot down by some lucky small-arms fire on Sixth and Weldon, near the city's unique downtown public pool, which for years now had been patronized almost exclusively by inner-city black kids, less for swimming than as a territorial prize. Still, a few more yards and NewsBird 9—you could read the logo, the helicopter on its side like a dead horse—could have made a water landing.

The camera pulled away fast; it was under fire, and the panicky audio cut back in. It was a mix of controlled professionalism and screaming and everything in between. Rudd was reminded of those cockpit tapes they sometimes release after a commercial jet goes down, unintelligible noises underscored on the nightly news by superimposed translations, as if the FAA was saying, This is what we hope they were saying. No underscores here, just the noises. Last shot was the copter pulling out, evidently unharmed, before the broadcast came back to an anchor seated at a desk. The morning commute's not looking so good. Back to you, Bob.

Behind the anchor—a man more weary than startled—was a state map with little flame icons sprouting from two of the state's three major cities. The anchor—his tie had been loosened and Rudd realized he had never seen this feature on an anchor before—spat out the names of these cities along with a few random statistics. Then a video effect caused the state map to be sucked into its smaller place in a national map, which now occupied the screen.

Brief exclamations popped about the room. It was important to acknowledge this stark, bicolored, line-drawn graphic, cogently more terrifying than the live video from moments before. Some fifteen or twenty little flame icons shadowed city dots across the map. Popcorn, thought Rudd, like their vocal reaction had been a sound track for this static image.

"There's another one!" said Miles, pointing at the screen as if the existing little flame icons were absorbed, understood, and accepted and this new little flame icon was the real news. True though, there was another one, and the city not so darn big, a place in fact where one might justify one's relocation by pointing out the indigenous security, the small-town atmosphere, the kids-walk-to-school-and-sometimes-we-even-forget-to-lock-the-door-at-nightness of the place.

Back to the anchor, the map zapped from full-screen but still looming over his shoulder, like it ain't that easy. The man was listening intently to audio coming over his earpiece, had his hand up to it as the other hand received sheets of yellow paper torn hastily from what they call a legal pad and presumably carrying details of late-breaking events. The information age.

No commercials, thought Rudd.

I need a fucking drink, thought Langston, and he poured himself one.

My parents, thought Jill, apropos of the position of one of the little flame icons she saw on the screen.

"What are we going to do about him?" asked Fenton of Rudd without benefit of a gesture, the object of inquiry being fairly obvious.

Miles and Osmond pretended to be too absorbed in the TV to acknowledge and therefore participate in this, and perhaps they were. Langston was absorbed in his drink but otherwise willing to be of service.

Rudd half-heartedly looked around for the busboy before saying, "I guess you, me, and Langston can drag him into the freezer."

"Sort of what I was thinking," agreed Fenton.

Langston nodded, gulping. Such was McTeague.

Though Rudd would have preferred her to retire to the ladies' room (or now *lady's* room), Jill took a seat in one of the nearer booths and waited to wipe up the blood. As he moved behind the bar he caught a glimpse of the television. An intrepid reporter on the street talking with a local black religious figure; in the background the crowd, not missing their big chance to be on TV, hammed it up for the camera as though this was merely another drive-by shooting being covered. All those faces, smiling, some holding up the fruits of the morning's looting, one guy with a Macintosh computer for chrissake, this is what Miles and Osmond couldn't tear themselves away from, thought Rudd. He and Fenton exchanged a glance, and Langston came 'round quickly to meet them.

Of the three thick net-like rubber mats behind the bar at Tony's the bartender occupied most of the third one or the one nearest the front of the restaurant, deepest in the bar. If the other two were removed first it would make for an easier drag—magic carpet—but when Langston, instantly and silently apprehending the situation, turned around to clear the path he found himself anticipated, Miles and Osmond bearing away a mat apiece. Well then, he thought, good for Rudd; we're all here.

Rudd and Fenton each grabbed a corner of the third mat; thus the body was dragged feet-first over the greasy tile. It was easy going, and Langston knew that he would amount to too many cooks so he stood by. Jill watched the whole thing. She didn't blink, didn't look away. She knew it would be better for her not to. She was in school. They all were, but she was the one who knew it first.

One nice thing about the rubber mat was that it protected the body from any unfortunate head bumps around corners.

The trip to the freezer transpired without incident (insofar as it could, given the circumstances), and it wasn't three minutes before the dead man was laid to rest in the far corner of the mercifully far-cornered freezer. Langston manned the door and watched Rudd and Fenton leave mat and all to kingdom come. The noises now were as follows: buzz from freezer lamp; outside gunfire; click of freezer-door latch as Langston let it slip; nothing from Rudd and Fenton; continuing coverage being watched by Miles and Osmond; plastic bottle being struck against plastic bucket as Jill searched the cleaning-supply closet for something to take up the already dried blood from the bartender's chest (with a cursory look ahead to something gentle enough to serve as laundry soap). One block away a yellow traffic-signal box clicked, illuminating a *WALK* sign—as absurd as the trash basket over which it loomed beneath the sparkling sunny sky. This annoyed a man nearby, who fired six rounds from his 1911 clone forty-five at the box. He ran off; the box continued to operate; those shots changed nothing, and the sound of them, like a tree falling, went unacknowledged in Tony's.

Langston, it would be recalled later in seemingly endless discussion of the incident, was either just closing or double-checking the latching of the freezer door when the fiercest barrage of gunfire they had experienced to date hammered the rear door. Rudd, Fenton, and Jill, all still in the kitchen with Langston (though not near him), instinctively sought cover, as did Miles and Osmond though they were back in front and in no immediate danger. Rudd was fairly certain that the door would hold up, and he was right;

the few bullets that entered the room managed the trick via lucky landings on a previously weakened seam near a long-sealed hole originally intended as a night depository location of the S&L that Tony's was originally intended to be. Sounded like two or three guys emptying as many clips, not unlike what they'd been hearing all through the night only closer, prompting Rudd to realize that what they *had* been hearing and by now pretty much ignoring was in each case probably a terrifying experience to someone somewhere. Little flame icons.

"Don't worry," he shouted to Jill, wrapped on the far side of a steel dishwasher and more or less out of harm's way. "That door will take a lot."

"Well it's getting it," she responded, rather pluckily, he thought, suddenly aroused either despite or because of the situation.

The pop of the aerosol can of Brite 'n' White cleaning solvent, which the busboy knew could cut through grease like nobody's business, was a noise for Langston's ears alone. And he didn't scream, merely began rubbing his eyes and waiting for a lull in the shooting so that he might make his way to the sink and rinse them. He didn't try to open them; he was a smarter man than that, and he tried to limit his rubbing to the surrounding area, that he might remove the excess fluid that began burning his skin as sort of an underscore to the unspeakable things it was doing to his eyes, open at the time of the small explosion and inches from the can.

"Jesus Christ!" said Rudd as he caught a glimpse of Langston's face during the quick post-shooting inventory of his companions that was well on its way to becoming habitual. "Your face!" And he was upon him, leading him to the sink.

But no one knew yet the real damage, that Langston was blind, though the latter began to suspect it when he hit the sink and tried to open his eyes only to realize that they were already open. What Rudd was responding to was the accumulation of blood from the little cuts caused by can shrapnel which had peppered Langston's face, nothing too bad or deep but looking that way due to being spread about by the latter's hands. This became apparent under the cooling water, surprisingly efficacious in the relief it granted from the sting and burn. What also became apparent first to Rudd, then to Jill, who had to turn away from the sight, was the condition of Langston's eyeballs.

"Do you think we could try for a hospital?" he asked.

A siren wailed in the distance, and for an absurd moment Rudd wondered who had called 911. "I don't think you'd make the triage cut," he answered.

"True enough," said Langston, and Rudd marveled at the man.

Jill cried and went to fetch a bottle of scotch without being told to. Or even asked. Fetch.

Hours later as the afternoon burned beyond the security shutters the group was collected at the bar, all except for the busboy, who remained unnoticed in the kitchen and would have in any case been indignant at being considered one of the group. So would most of the group, for that matter. These hours had passed as if through a plenum, bearing with them a feeling of compression that permitted Langston's blindness to become part of the group's reality in far less time than any of them would have predicted. Even Langston accepted his condition readily, holding on only through some learned sense of commitment to his body, to the vaguest of hopes that his blindness might be temporary, his eyesight only an alcoholic blackout away.

On the benches near the windows at the front of Tony's was where Langston lay. It would become a favorite place for him, those benches. He was fiddling with his gun, loading and unloading it from the new boxes of hollow points that he and Rudd had retrieved from his car late the previous night, learning about feeling things with his fingers and secretly enjoying this new limitation as if it represented a chance to play life again under a new set of rules.

Miles and Osmond glanced nervously at him, at Rudd, and at each other, watching the direction of the Beretta's barrel as it moved between the hands of this blind man. Too embarrassed to say anything themselves, they hoped that Rudd might suggest to Langston that he put the gun down, but Rudd looked entirely unconcerned, lost in his own world, their world.

"Say there, Langston," decided Miles after downing his drink for fortification, "where'd you get so much ammo?" He looked at Osmond, smiled broadly so everyone would know that this was purely conversational to pass the time of day and in no way was it anything at which offense should be taken.

Osmond smiled back, nodding eagerly so that Miles wanted to groan.

"My car," said Langston. "Guess it's yours now, Rudd."

"The car?" said Osmond, and everybody wondered if he was being cute or did he really want to know; his face offered no clue.

"That too I suppose," said Langston, characteristically trying to be pleasant and assuming the best. "But I was referring to these rounds. They're nine-mm, and if I recall correctly Rudd's Glock 19 is the only gun that takes this caliber, other than my Beretta that is."

"And who gets that?" said Rudd, staring hard at Langston, hoping for a penetration of sorts.

"*I* keep that," Langston told him, surprisingly meeting his eyes though this man saw nothing.

"Good," said Rudd. "Then you'll need the rounds. I have ammo in my car if I need it."

"Well who doesn't," said Miles. "I do. I know he does," indicating Osmond with his thumb. "What about you, Fenton?" Then, off the latter's nod. "See. But a lot of good it does us in here, and I sure as hell am not going out there to get it. I can't believe you guys went. Sort of reckless, don't you think, endangering everybody like that? If I'd been awake I'd have stopped you." He paused, uncomfortable with the sound of that and uncomfortable with the idea of toning it down. "Or at least tried."

"We went out to close the security shutters—has to be done from the outside." Rudd stood, but it turned out only to be so he could pour another drink. "Langston's car was right there and he thought it would be a good idea to have some extra ammo. I agreed." He sat back down. "Sorry if you'd rather not be left out of these things, Miles. Next time I'll be sure to wake you."

They fell silent, uncomfortable flirting with contention, knowing it wouldn't help their situation. Jill felt like an observer and didn't dare say a word. But she wanted to speak. She didn't have anything to say really, just the need to speak, the need to get in now before it was too late, before she was shut out for the duration. Duration.

"It would be nice to have a little breathing room," said Fenton, breaking the silence. "I only have two clips on me, one in the gun."

They all agreed via nods and grunts.

"So go get it," said Jill, and the pronouncement was, to say the least, galvanizing.

Fenton looked at Rudd. That's when it happened, the exact moment when it became certain that they would attempt to recover all the ammo from their cars. Even Miles and Osmond knew they would be involved, and Osmond was frightened and Miles was ready. Inside he knew: he would grow readier by the hour, by the day too. Miles liked to shoot his gun. He did like that.

"What the fuck," said Miles. He wanted to get a jump on the quorum, but he ended up startling Osmond more than impressing the others.

Rudd and Fenton were still on each other's eyes. "We could do it," said Fenton to his friend's already nodding face. It was one of those slow nods geared to appear contemplative.

"I bet we could," said Rudd to Fenton. "I bet we could," said Rudd to the others.

"We'd want to go in the very early morning, that's when things are likely to be quietest. Say right before the sun comes up."

The men nodded, concurring with Fenton's sound logic.

"Well my alarm's on," said Osmond for no apparent reason.

Miles turned to him with a quizzical squint. "Um, gee, Osmond, then I suppose your car will be pretty safe out there. I bet the looters are giving it a wide berth," he said, hurting the man.

"I only meant that it'll be hard to get into it quietly. It'll chirp when I turn it off."

"No," said Langston from the bench. "Best set it off, break a window even. Nobody will notice that. We've been hearing car alarms all night—maybe our own for all we know. In any case the chirp of turning one off will almost certainly attract more hostile attention than if you sound like just another punk."

Punk? thought Rudd. Sounded funny coming from Langston. Guess when you're blind you can say anything. He said, "My Caddy's parked in back. We could hit it no problem. You're in front, right?" He wondered if Osmond was the only one here with an alarm, but then he knew Fenton had one. Maybe Rudd was the only one here *without* one. He decided to let it drop, hating the way that such a thing might be a status issue to a jerk like Miles.

Fenton nodded.

Rudd turned to Miles and Osmond. "How about you guys?"

"On the street, not far," said Miles.

"Me too," said Osmond. "But I'm on the other side. It's a red Z, only four months old. They sell 'em red, but mine's custom lacquer. You'll spot it right away. It's real distinctive."

Miles considered telling him to shut up but then thought better of it and had another drink instead. Rudd wondered why he was the only one who parked in back. He had always parked in back and assumed that all the regulars did, but now that he thought about it he realized that he'd never seen anybody but the valets back there. Could be that it was off-limits back there and Tony had given the word to let him slide as a valued customer. Could also be that the valets figured he wasn't worth the bother.

"Langston's is done, so we don't have to worry about that. I say we go before dawn tomorrow morning," said Rudd as if tossing it out for a vote.

"What do you drive, Langston?" Osmond wanted to know or at least wanted to know more than he wanted to agree to the proposal on the bar. After he said this he was proud of himself for talking so casually with a blind man, and he hoped the men had noticed and the woman too (he didn't care about the busboy).

"Black Saab," Langston told him. He was smelling a bullet and sounded distracted to Osmond, who considered the question more interesting than the smell of a bullet and was frantically searching his head to remember what cost more, the Nissan or the Saab. "900 Turbo convertible."

Maybe the Saab, feared Osmond. "Nice family car, I guess," he said. Smelling bullets. Gross.

"Well you'll get to see it in a few hours," said Rudd condescendingly.

Without being polled Miles said tersely, "I'm in."

"Okay. Got a plan, Fenton?" Rudd was self-satisfied with how he'd coddled everyone into agreement, and now he wanted to keep his momentum by openly seeking Fenton's counsel about the particulars.

Fenton thought for a moment before saying, "Only that we should do it all at once. I think it's imperative to our security in here that the door be opened a minimum number of times, not only to minimize the risk of someone rushing it, but also to keep anybody from expecting it to open and setting up an ambush. The fewer times it's opened the less chance of it being seen open."

"I don't follow," said Miles.

"No, he's right," said Rudd.

"Absolutely," echoed Langston, now touching his tongue to the same bullet he'd been smelling a few moments before, playing out the whole procedure as if he were trying to get a handle on how to ingest some inscrutable new drug, something beyond cocaine or Pepsi, the choice of a new generation.

"What we'll do is all go to our own car at the same time," said Rudd. "That will not only be less conspicuous than traveling in a group, but it will also minimize the time we spend outside." Thinking he saw a nod of approval from her, he looked over to Jill, but she was still, merely listening without comment.

"So nobody gets cover?" demanded Miles.

Fenton piped in with, "No. It's not worth it. If we get into a cover situation we're probably fucked anyhow—"

He was interrupted by a sudden and insistent banging on the outer security shutter. Muffled though it was through the various barriers, an urgent plea could also be distinguished, running under the percussion like a poorly played snare.

Everyone froze, not wanting to admit to themselves or to each other that not only was this somebody who needed help but that they were powerless to act. There would be no way to articulate this without sounding like a self-serving coward, and truth be told some of these men just wanted the sound to go away, perhaps wouldn't help if they could. The first four eyes to meet were Rudd's and Jill's; he looked at her for a cue, a catalyst to induce a reaction in the glimmer of heroism he was experiencing, a feeling somewhere between the base of his penis and the back of his throat. When he looked up she was waiting for him, looking at him, and his cue came in the form of a single shake of her head. Slight—left, right—point of the nose: No.

He looked at Fenton. "Poor son of a bitch," he said. Fenton.

"We don't know that," said Miles. "He could be bla—one of them."

"Black or white, the guy needs help," said Langston.

Then the shutter rattled briefly, struck by bullets, and there was no more pounding and there was no more screaming and there was no more discussion of the incident but for Miles's observation that black or white he was dead now.

"But I guess we don't know that either," he added, "the poor son of a bitch."

When they finished with that and the appropriate time had been spent doing that and thinking about that and regretting that and whatever else they felt might be required of themselves by one another it was decided that the foray to the vehicles for ammo would proceed and that Rudd and Fenton's ideas on how to conduct it would prevail over Miles's objections. For Rudd it was a seminal moment in his command (as he had come to think of it). For Fenton it was a noteworthy intercourse in his relationship with Rudd, and under a renewal of distant gunfire in the surrounding neighborhood he felt grateful that he'd never married. He was a single man, Fenton, and his life was wherever he put it.

Jill's perspective was from behind the coffee machines at the back of the bar, but with the shutters closed the place was smaller and quieter, so it didn't seem so far away from the men, who were fairly spread out anyway. In fact the room really did appear to have closed in slightly, compressed, she thought. Then she thought, This is a different issue, this is a piece of trouble that will not go away so I might as well deal with it later when I know more about what this all is. She was struck by the uniform appearance of the men. Each one sat behind a bottle clutching his glass like so many game show contestants standing by with hands on buzzers. Even the labels were all turned outward as if by design. It positively looked like some bizarre alky taste test or maybe a panel of debaters at a drunk convention. What was it with these guys? Somewhere, somehow she knew in her heart of hearts that, prevailing wisdom notwithstanding, money ought to buy at least a modicum of happiness. Yet these men, for all their bread, didn't look very happy. At times there were glimmers of boys in the faces, not men acting like boys but rather men who had been boys. It was good for her to catch these moments, for they provided a path to compassion, and she began to wait for them, watch for them; in time she would come to live for them, those boys who flitted in and out of men's faces.

The television hummed into the evening, and though no one watched or listened with any real commitment it is unlikely that any of them considered turning it off, any more than they would have considered turning off the clock on the wall, their watches, or the interruption-of-service recording one heard over the unavailing phone line. There were clicks on that line too. Jill was tired. She'd been standing in the same place for hours; the TV screen had become for her nothing more than an abstract light source, suggesting imaginary objects per the whim of her semi-consciousness, both sides now and pixilated clouds drifting over a nice girl like her and a place like this, a beta citizen in an alpha state. Hard not to think about the threat in a roomful of penises she simply doesn't want anything to do with, so well-off white guys might at least provide a balance of power, which would keep her safe, but the looks will wax ever more lecherous and the thoughts will spark and linger time to lie down in a booth turn off the coffee maker that bra take a nap now and wash clothes tomorrow. She tried to focus on the television, searching for an update, a you-are-here arrow in the map of the apocalypse, but this simple grasp at information was beyond her for now. She focused on the booth, focused mentally. Then she walked over to it and lay down and then she was asleep.

Rudd, midway into a no-problem-yet drunk, watched surreptitiously her departure from the bar while pretending to ponder Langston's position on the advisability of federally sponsored urban growth programs. This was solid old reliable drunk conversation, and everyone was indulging up to their eyeballs because it was familiar and relaxing; it came easy to them and it was what they would be doing right now even if there were no riot. A nice victory in a time like this, to be doing what you'd be doing anyway. Rudd liked looking at Jill and in fact had originally begun conversing with Langston because he assumed his wayward glances would go unnoticed. But it turned out that his verbal responses echoed quite accurately the degree of his attention, and he soon discovered that the conversation had to be conducted just like any other, with stolen glances and covert yawns. With Jill retired Rudd assembled a response to Langston's droning. He was starting to care about having this conversation, Rudd was, feeling fire in his pontifications and growing impatient to advance his own theories. He knew this meant he was upping the stakes, moving from drunk to drunker, and he fucking loved it.

Halfway up the bar Fenton, Miles, and Osmond were engaged in their own conversation, the latter the drunkest of the lot if one were to split hairs, trying hard to keep up with the television as a way to briefly enter the conversation, to infuse it with new information, updates from the world at large like so many multicolored candy sprinkles falling on a ponderous dollop of whipped cream. Drinking made Osmond hungry, and he secretly suspected that when drunk he could eat with impunity. Sure, perhaps he's taking in a few extra calories but certainly the alcohol must be blasting away all that lethal cholesterol from his arteries just as the Wet-Naps at Kentucky Fried Chicken so facilely remove the chicken grease from his fingers.

Fenton, sipping a J&B soda and predisposed to stick with it as *what* he drinks now *that* he drinks, nonetheless made a show of sampling, at Miles's behest, small splashes of the various scotches carried at Tony's. Miles pushed hard for Cutty Sark, this being his scotch, though at this moment he clutched a tall glass containing a Long Island Iced Tea hybrid padded with liqueurs and considered by its creator to be somewhat more expedient than Cutty Sark and somewhat less deserving of careful attention (though he gulped all his drinks with the same celerity). Fenton found himself taking to the copious refills pretty well. He amazed himself with his own tolerance, as if it had been latent inside of him, ready at any time to roll into his hand, ready for use with no period of nascency. And damn lucky too, that, because it didn't look as though he'd be given much time to get himself up to speed with the other men. This is where he lived now—that much was clear—and he needed to be a part of it, needed to be here for Rudd, to find a good stool from which to view the apocalypse. J&B would be the call—that too was clear—no whiskey, no silly drunk man's Cutty Sark or gooey liqueurs, just stand-up scotch and guns. Fenton found himself perturbed at the way Rudd had been sneaking glances at that waitress all evening, and even now as she slept he kept trying to get a look at her, though he would have to look straight through Fenton to see her. When their eyes met Fenton smiled and Rudd nodded, tacked on a small eye-roll as if he'd been trying to catch Fenton's eye to provide this light commentary on how the discussion with Langston was going. Fenton saw through that, but he also appreciated the effort. He was drunk. He desperately wanted to be a priority.

"Look!" Osmond yelped, pointing at the television and knocking over his glass in the process. Glass breaks along rim. Vodka seeks fissures in slate-covered bar. Men are troubled by notion of lost liquor but don't yet know why. Clip full of bullets purges into sky not forty feet from the back door. Goes unnoticed by all but busboy, who turns in his sleep, frightened and alone in the kitchen and bearing bad dreams.

No one looks at the television except for Langston, who can't see it anyway, and of course Osmond, who was already looking and doesn't appear interested in following up on his entreaty; or maybe he was merely thinking aloud.

"Now try the Cutty again," enjoined Miles, indicating, even pushing gently forth an inch or two, a rocks glass that had come to be the basis for comparison in the lecture-as-delivered.

Fenton obliged, happy to be past the John Begg scotch that Miles had just given him. He began to suspect that Miles was stacking the deck, pouring the worst scotches right before the next control sip of Cutty and the better scotches as a preface to Fenton's own glass of J&B, his basis for comparison in the lecture-as-received. "It's better than that last stuff," he opined, "but I still like the J&B."

"What do you know from scotch?" demanded Miles rhetorically, much annoyed at this intransigence. He plucked the glass of Cutty from Fenton's hand and downed it angrily. "You decide you want to be a scotch drinker and I invest all this time and effort in showing you what's what and you don't even want to listen!"

"I don't see what you're getting so upset about. It's not like I asked you."

"That's not the point." Miles paused, constructing the point in his head. "When a man reaches that stage in his life where he's ready to call scotch his drink he ought to be able to discern a little quality. That's the whole point of scotch! Otherwise he was never ready to begin with. Or he's just faking."

"This is stupid," said Fenton, knowing it was. "Besides, Langston doesn't drink that Cutty shit," he added, too drunk to stop himself.

"Langston's a spoiled rich kid grown up. And now he's blind."

"What does *that* have to do with anything?"

"He's used to having what he wants, not what he *should* have."

Fenton tried this on in an effort to reveal it. "So I should drink a scotch I don't like because it's better for me?"

"Better in a quality sense. Start now when it's all new to you, and you'll develop a taste for it. Don't you see? This is a perfect opportunity for you to learn to like a quality scotch. I mean, you've got to start from scratch anyway, so why not develop yourself into a real scotch drinker? Believe me, you'll thank me in years to come. Just ask Osmond."

But this last suggestion was forgotten as quickly as it was spoken, and not because Osmond didn't even drink scotch, a detail that didn't occur to either man. They fell to silence and brooded over their respective glasses, both ready to move along to new business. Fenton realized that Langston had fallen asleep, lay supine on the bench. Rudd appeared either lost in thought or half asleep himself. Osmond was glassy-eyed over his newly poured martini, locked onto the television screen.

"Oh fuck. I don't know. Guess it's you if it's you and me if it's me," Miles deduced rather nonsensically. "We agree to disagree," he clarified, extending his hand.

Fenton took the proffered palm, and they shook hands protractedly and with genuine (if ephemeral) affection. "At least we won't be stepping on each other's toes when the well starts to run dry," he said.

And that shut them both up in a hell of a hurry.

Day 3

T he first thing Osmond saw when he opened his eyes was the television screen. Tape he'd seen last night but he was frightened nonetheless, and he jumped—more of a convulsion—so hard that he knocked the table of the booth he was sleeping in and sent a glass rolling off the side. It shattered and Rudd snapped to and the two men looked at each other.

"I fell asleep," said Rudd, checking his watch. He settled back slightly. "Good, it's only four-thirty. We'll still have time."

Fuck, thought Osmond. "I'm so fucking hung over. I was only getting up for another drink. You go back to sleep," he tried.

Rudd said nothing but did swing his legs onto the floor and began to yawn and stretch the sleep from his system.

"I guess I fell asleep too," said Osmond, standing to fetch a swallow of vodka. "Came over here to watch some TV, but not so close. You know?"

Rudd nodded, the easy way out.

"Right. So like that," sputtered Osmond, very, very nervous and making no sense.

Drunk, scared, thought Rudd.

Fenton had been right; it *was* quiet at this hour, as if the riots had settled into a schedule, dropped the pace and sought their own level, oozed like Osmond's vodka into the crevices, keeping a skim over the flat regions but leaving room for the high points of not-riot to peak through. Okay for now, but this was in fact a sign of a long haul.

"Your friend was right," said Osmond to Rudd. "I don't hear any shooting. Maybe it's all blowing over." He sipped his newly poured vodka, drained it, and felt some hope. "Maybe we should call this off and wait. We could make sure, because if it's gonna be over we don't want to risk our necks for nothing. Right?"

Osmond poured more vodka for himself. This annoyed Rudd more than the man's whining, though he couldn't yet say why. Keep it easy.

Silently Rudd walked over to where Fenton was slumped in a booth. He stopped short, as if remembering something, and turned back to the bar where Osmond stood. "I hope so, Osmond. That would be great, and I hope you're right. But I think we'll go just the same. Just in case. That way we'll be prepared." He patted Osmond on the back affectionately while grabbing the bottle of vodka with his other hand. "Need to borrow this for a second," he said.

Behind the bar he found the plastic bottle of tomato juice, but it smelled a little too organic and he poured it out. Under the bar were the large cans from which these bottles were filled, oversized cans with scaled-up labels that made them look like props from *Land of the Giants*, a television show from his childhood, a show that aired during the same years Rudd would find such cans in the family refrigerator. V8, those were, his father preferring that brand to the blander Campbell's Tomato Juice which Rudd now held in his larger-than-his-father's-was hand. He'd read somewhere that they were going to make a *Land of the Giants* movie, this when it seemed all they ever made anymore were movies based on terrible old television shows, the worse the better, like some guy hearing a joke wrong but laughing and repeating it anyway rather than appearing to have not *gotten* it. Those movie people thought bad equaled camp. Big cans of juice had given way to glass, then plastic, then glass again, because in the world of recycling some things were more equal than others, a lesson those movie people would do well to learn. We'd reached the evolutionary peak of packaging too quickly, faster anyhow than developments in parallel technologies would allow us to proceed. Or perhaps we wised up and caught a glimpse of the ennui implicit in that kind of dead end, extrapolated a Characteristic straight through a Downside and arrived at a Problem that allowed us to back down with honor. Such was the view from the peak, from the top of a big plastic bottle of V8, from the glory days of styrofoam when the hot side stayed hot and the cool side stayed cool. A *Land of the Giants* movie. . . . Rudd tasted copper in his mouth. He really couldn't say, as he glanced at the coverage of the apocalypse on the television screen, whether he'd rather be watching that or this right now.

Rudd poured a stiff bloody mary as Osmond looked on and wondered why it had to be from the vodka bottle *he'd* been drinking from and not one of the zillion others behind the bar. Rudd downed the drink and poured another one, which he carried past Osmond (not bothering to return the pilfered vodka, Osmond noticed but didn't mention) back to the booth where Fenton slept.

"Hey," he nudged.

Fenton half opened his eyes and groaned. "Oh God," he said.

"Drink this quick," Rudd told him.

"I did this once in college."

"Drink this."

"Swore I'd never do it again."

"No bullshit. Just drink it."

"I almost made it."

"You didn't even come close. Now are you going to drink this or are you going to spend the day moaning and puking?"

Fenton sat up and took the glass. "Both, would be my guess," he said.

Rudd watched approvingly as his friend downed the drink as quickly as possible. He figured Fenton wouldn't need too much instruction, not because he was experienced but because he'd watched Rudd do this many times at Hollydale. Fenton handed him the empty glass, and Rudd went to refill it.

"Shouldn't I be relatively sober, that is if we're still planning to go out to the cars this morning?"

"Oh we're going all right," said Rudd from the bar. "Just as soon as you get sober, which should be right after this drink."

"I'm not you, Rudd. It doesn't work that way with me, not yet anyway."

"It does when you're hung over. Better drunk than sick." He stopped what he was doing and announced loudly to the room, "Let's go men! C'mon, wake up! It'll be light soon and we can't have that."

Rudd smiled at the grimacing Fenton, who said, "Jesus, Rudd."

"Don't worry," said Rudd, still smiling and bearing the fresh drink. "Stick with me and hangovers will be a thing of the past."

"Fuck you, Rudd," squawked Miles from his booth.

"You too, Miles. Now get up."

Osmond, still at the bar, debated whether or not to make a drink for Miles. But it seemed different somehow, and he knew from experience that whenever he tried to do stuff like that it usually went badly. Jill sat up, looked around, and hurried off to the restroom. Langston hadn't moved, but Rudd saw that his eyes were open so he must be awake; then he wasn't so sure. Is Langston dead? And even if he's not, do blind people close their eyes at night?

"Langston, you awake?" Rudd said crisply, one vertebrate to another.

"Well my eyes are open, aren't they?"

"Just asking. I've got better things to do than gaze into your eyes, Langston," said Rudd, adding a chuckle so that everyone would take it right. Then he thought, God, I hope he wasn't really asking me.

Osmond said (and anyone could tell he was already loaded), "Yeah, they're open, but we thought you might be dead."

At this everyone laughed, which annoyed Rudd to no end. The busboy stood in the kitchen making himself a three-egg omelet, the smell of which reached Fenton, nauseating him. In the restroom Jill devised a sort of lock for the door by using a chair braced under the decorative brushed stainless-steel handle. She took off her shirt and approached the mirror with the idea of inspecting a pimple she had been tracking on her back, but like a slap in the face it occurred to her that she should have Langston's gun. It should have been offered to her, offered right away. That was all she thought about while she looked in the mirror, getting angrier and angrier. She stayed there for quite some time. If Rudd could have seen her, standing there in her bra, he most certainly would have had an erection.

In the kitchen, nothing left of the busboy's breakfast but the residual grease and odor, Rudd corralled the men near the back door. But it was Langston (getting a bit too comfortable, Rudd thought, with the privilege of blindness, which was quite frankly beginning to wear a little thin, and the others, Rudd was sure, would agree) who led things off with his calm intonation, insidiously insistent in its very lack of presumption, from the rear of the group.

"Just go," he said. "At this point the less thought put into this the better. I'll wait by the door, and if I hear trouble I'll fire some shots into the air as cover. You hear that, come running back. If you can."

Rudd then felt things generally turn to him, so he nodded before unbolting the door and pushing out. This was yes. Outside the night was still as fucking graffiti.

Miles was fourth out, and he turned control of the door over to Langston, who could and would go either way. Again Rudd nodded, and they dispersed. Rudd reached his Cadillac first, for his was the nearest car, parked behind the restaurant and not fifty feet from the door. He regretted this, wished that his had been the longest and riskiest of the four runs because it would have allowed him to push the issue harder than he had. As it was he had pretty much let Fenton and Langston have the show, but at least it was better than having Miles accuse him of having glass balls, something that jerk would no doubt come up with. It was so quiet that he felt silly running, until it occurred to him that if someone were out here waiting for the back door to open then Rudd would be the first target. There were plenty of ideal sniper locations with a great view of this lot; he hoped the others appreciated that.

His Caddy looked pretty good, at least from this side. A brick rested on the hood, having evidently bounced on and dented a few places, but no windows were broken—small miracle—and Rudd realized that he'd need to pull out his keys and unlock the door to get in. Annoying, this, because he always approached his car with his keys in hand. It pissed him off that he should neglect this simple idiosyncrasy at the very moment it would be most appropriate. Of course he could *afford* any alarm he wanted; he just didn't want one. Carry around a fucking remote control in your pocket all day. They didn't have those things when this car was built. Show a little style. Chirp chirp! Fucking pompous faggots. He put the key into the driver's door lock and almost opened it before remembering how it always makes a rusty squeal. So far so good, but best use the passenger side. Nimbly he passed around the rear of the car, opened the door, and felt the cool invitation of his Cadillac's interior.

The other men, having started their runs more or less in a group due to the relative proximity of their cars, broke swiftly apart as they turned from the rear parking area into the alley that ran alongside Tony's to the street. Things took on an every-man-for-himself feel, a thought better left to the deep dark realm of retrospective solitude. Of these men Miles made his car first, a white Mercedes parked not far from the outlet of the alley and on the same side of the street. It had been hit hard and looked it, what with most of the windows broken and the passenger door standing open. Miles's first reaction was anger that his alarm had not sounded, but he wouldn't have noticed it if it had so he really didn't know. One of so many alarms, he spent a moment in vain trying to parse the almost constant dialog of alarms that had underscored these many hours, trying to isolate which had been his and what he'd been doing right then. His stereo was missing. He felt violated, same as he did all the other times his stereo had been stolen, once in this very neighborhood, and he wondered if that would be a problem with the insurance. There was a small explosion in the east and the sky lit up briefly, a trailer for the sun, a coming attraction. Miles gasped; though he could hear other men at their cars, or at least knew they were there, he felt very alone. His face caught a chill, glistening in the crisp night air.

Fenton's Lexus, half a block down on the same side of the street, looked okay except for a small object resting on top of the car. As he drew closer (circumspectly, caution being prescribed when dealing with an unforeseen circumstance such as this) he also noticed the rear passenger-side vent window had been shattered, like some street thug thought it was business as usual and went in the professional way. Guy was probably in and out in something like fifteen seconds, disappeared down an alley with Fenton's Alpine under his arm, dodging the more opportunistic looters. Close up Fenton was able to identify what rested on his roof. It was—absurdly—a half-eaten hot dog sitting in a small pleated-paper tray, so neatly that it seemed to have been carefully placed there. Perhaps the roof of his car had served as spectator seating for whatever had been going on out here. Inside, he noticed, his alarm indicator light was pulsing at twice its normal rate, a signal to its owner that it had gone off for ninety seconds before rearming itself. Fenton, whose condo sat above a parking garage that seemed perpetually to ring with ignored car alarms, especially at five in the morning, had insisted on this feature when purchasing the unit. He was not a man to fuck with the peace, and he paused after instinctively reaching for his remote. His fingers played over the car keys, the little plastic box to which they were attached like little pocket convicts. He remembered the earlier conversation: Langston would have him set it off. Good advice. It all made perfect sense. Years with car alarms and he was the only person he knew who hadn't accidentally set off his own alarm at one time or another. Fenton was proud of that record. One little chirp. His fingers caressed the remote. You have your logic and you have your gut, he thought. But for a small explosion in the east things were quiet. He stood there in the night, reached out and lightly touched the hot dog with the tip of his index finger.

Z. Far side of the street, and even with all this bad shit going down (one might say if one were black), Osmond felt the same tingle of pride he always felt when approaching his car. Red. Or even just catching sight of it. He surveyed the surrounding cars and it didn't look good; almost every car had been fucked with in some way, and despite his already labored breathing Osmond quickened his trot and his belly filled with anxiety. He was scared to be out here and he hoped he wouldn't piss himself or worse. An explosion in the east didn't help that situation at all. Z looked okay as he approached it, but that would be too much to hope for. Z's other side must be fucked. He ran up to the car and circled it completely, barely slowing. And fuck if it wasn't totally untouched. That fucking alarm really paid off, he thought, and a smile overtook his face as he gazed at Z's interior, his reflection on the placid glass. The red armed-indicator light of his alarm dinked and poppled on the tip of his reflected nose, almost tickled, hee-hee. So you can't have everything you want, fuckers, thought Osmond as he pulled his keys from his pocket. He hit the little green disarm button on his remote, and the single chirp of his alarm rang out through the quiet streets and alleys that crissed and crossed about the smoldering neighborhood. Now that's a reassuring sound.

One hundred yards away (as the drunk weaves) two men sat with their backs resting against a Dumpster. Between them lay a third man, prone and with a cheap steak knife rising and falling between his shoulder blades with the diminishing breathy gags of expiration. Other wounds peppered this man, wounds from the same knife and bullet wounds too, the latter having brought him down and the former being inflicted as mostly sport and to settle the argument about what kind of noise a knife makes when inserted into human flesh. His attackers were so occupied sorting cash and credit cards, bickering like kids over Halloween candy, that they didn't even notice when the breathing stopped. In any case the show was getting old for them, and since neither could believe that this free-for-all would last forever they had developed something of a let's-move-on consensus. One was working hard on selling the other on a you-take-the-cards-and-I'll-take-the-cash arrangement, and amazingly enough he felt he was getting close, there being one born every minute, when the chirp of a car alarm seized their common attention.

"What the fuck," said Cash, almost smiling.

Cards's hand fell to his waistband, to the white plastic grip of his forty-five. He was just plain glad to be there.

It was lucky that Langston had that extra nine-mm ammo because the only thing Rudd had in the Caddy right now was three boxes of 380 rounds for his Walther. They were in the glove compartment, where he also normally kept extra nine-mm as well but had used them (loaned them, actually) during an impromptu stop at the firing range the week before. Promise of a quick replacement from Maxwell, the acquaintance at the range who had borrowed them, prevented Rudd from buying more. Lesson learned. He dropped into the passenger side and opened the glove compartment. The 380 rounds were still there; he knew they would be. All was quiet except for that small explosion in the east, and that was nothing. Everything was going fine. He rose from the car, heard the chirp of an alarm. Paused.

Though the passenger door was already open Miles walked up to the driver's door and inserted the key into the lock—the only way to open it, despite the fact that the window was shattered. He eased the door open, and safety glass rained onto the pavement. In fact there was glass all over the seat, so much that he couldn't safely sit in it as he'd planned. He found a clear place to rest his palm and leaned into the car to access the console, knowing before he opened it that it would be empty. It was. Except for some gum wrappers (Trident Freshmint) and small sample vials of men's colognes (Aramis, Krizia Umo, which Miles always called Curious Homo, and a Calvin Klein, which was missing its promotional folder so he wasn't sure which fragrance but was pretty sure it was Calvin Klein though it wasn't worth reading the tiny type on the vial to find out, not now anyway), it was empty. Fuck, he thought, so now when I run out I'll have to use that peashooter of Langston's. A car alarm chirped down the street. Osmond, thought Miles absently, but he didn't look up and he didn't think about it again.

The hot dog rolled out of its bun and pleated-paper tray across half of Fenton's Lexus's roof, leaving mustard kisses at intervals of (approximately) $\pi H - M/2$, where H represents the diameter of the hot dog and M the width of the mustard dollop. Such a tiny little nudge—a tap really, barely made contact with the little fucker. Fenton stood there and tried to get over his frustration at himself. He knew it was insignificant, this hot dog incident, and he tried to get over it. Past it. Over. Move along. This wasn't like him at all, and he knew that the whole situation of being in Tony's and what was going on outside was getting to him. He was cracking maybe, and this made him even angrier. Just then he heard an alarm chirp off, and it shook him back to reality, back to the street at least. Fenton looked down the street and saw Osmond standing some ways off on the other side, addressing his red Nissan with his remote. Well big deal. Nobody really could expect that buffoon to follow orders anyway, not even Rudd. It was dead out here, no one around to notice an alarm chirp off. A tree falling in the woods: for all intents and purposes it didn't even make a noise. Spurious, he knew, but there was mustard all over his Lexus now. Fenton fingered his own remote. Fuck it, he thought and pointed it at the car. He pushed the button—chirp—like an echo.

For the second time in less than a minute Cash and Cards were surprised by an improbable sound.

"What The Fuck!" said Cash.

Cards decided, "Oh. Oh, wait a minute. Somebody's fucking around." But he didn't look very convinced. In fact he looked a little frightened, or at least ill-prepared for such a contingency. "I say we forget it," he added while pulling the knife out of the back of the man they had killed.

The man groaned and the knife made a slurping noise.

"Hoo hoo hoo hooo," wowed the men in unison, wide-eyed and full of wonderment.

"Now *that's* the sound I was talkin' about," said Cash. He took a beat to enjoy his moment. Then: "Let's go check this shit out. It sounds like a fucking CA meeting letting out."

Cards laughed, but he didn't get it.

Osmond felt the two-sided discomfort of his twin Smiths as he lowered himself into the driver's seat of Z. The guns pinched into him under the hug of the custom seat against his bulk, so much so that he usually removed them for driving. He wouldn't be here long though, so he put up with the press of steel and reached under the driver's seat for the four boxes of forty-four-mag rounds he kept there. He managed to wiggle out three of the boxes in fairly short order, but the fourth gave him some trouble and ended up requiring the full and variform suite of Osmond's capabilities before finally yielding to a simultaneous grunt and groin thrust backed with a sweat-lubricated hand held as horizontally as possible. The box joined the others in his lap. Osmond went *Whew.* He looked up, like waiting at a red light maybe. Two men stood watching him, not four feet from his startled nose.

Cash and Cards looked at this fat white fuck as if he were the best pork roast in the whole meat counter. He was so big and stupid looking that neither man had bothered to draw his gun, though Cards still held the bloody steak knife he'd extracted from his previous encounter with a not-so-fat white fuck.

"Let's just gut him," he said to his companion.

They glanced at each other, Cash and Cards did, because it felt like the right time to giggle and put a little sporty spin on the situation. But in truth they simply felt a bad vibe and needed the companionship. When their eyes met they knew that something was off, very wrong in fact. Then a tremendous crash stunned everybody as Osmond fired three shots from each revolver through the windshield of Z.

When Osmond opened his eyes the men were gone, and when he rose from Z he saw the men were on the ground. One was way dead shot through the head. The other was seriously fucked up, his belly all bloody and breathing quick and hard like some pre-D.O.A. on *America's Most Videoed Home Eviscerations.*

He shot that man once through the head. Then he holstered his weapons, retrieved the four boxes of ammo from the floor of Z, and began walking back to Tony's. Then he ran.

Fenton knew he was fucking up during the infinitesimal interval between the moment his finger was committed to depressing the alarm remote button and the moment the remote button could actually be described as pressed. Then it was done and there was no going back so the only thing to do was to go forward and, hopefully, fail to fuck up again. The one hundred spare rounds of forty-caliber ammunition he carried were in two boxes in an emergency road repair kit in the trunk of the Lexus, right in the hollow of an orange reflective triangle and concealed from casual inspection by a Need Help Call Police fold-out dashboard sun protector that always made Fenton think of the back cover of *Mad* magazine (though Rudd appeared downright dimwitted when Fenton tried to explain this to him, as if the man had never handled a *Mad* magazine). And now with the mustard. Not that that was Rudd's fault or even had anything to do with him, but still it rankled. He opened his trunk and popped the lid off the emergency road repair kit, dug out the ammo and put a box in each of his jacket's side pockets, and lowered the lid of the Lexus's trunk. He heard shots, which at first didn't register as something that required his attention, so quickly had he become inured to the sounds of the civil unrest (or were they simply sounds of civil unrest now, as in all?). Then there was that feeling that too had become a fact of life, that feeling that there was a problem at hand, and he moved up midway against the side of his car. Then Osmond was running toward, if not at, him, running hell-bent for election back to Tony's.

"Osmond!" yelled Fenton, "What is it?"

Osmond looked at him, made a frantic gesture with his arms that could have been interpreted as *hurry up and follow me* if it weren't so ridiculously cartoonish, and ran on.

Then there was another figure—Miles, it turned out to be—running toward them, away from Tony's.

"Cover Me!" he screamed, waving his Colt in the air as if this were the universal sign for *Cover Me!*

Fenton obligingly looked around for something to shoot at. Osmond took a few more steps before freezing in his tracks. Miles spun around and ducked in between two cars. Taking up position, was the phrase that sprang into Fenton's head as he watched Miles squat down and aim his weapon in

the direction from which he had come. Osmond did what
Miles did, only between Fenton's Lexus and the car behind
it. Fenton dithered a moment before following suit by squat-
ting in front of his Lexus as opposed to behind it next to
Osmond. This felt like the more military—if arbitrary—course
of action.

Stepped away from his Caddy, Rudd did. Cocked his
head. Heard another chirp. Paused. That would be two then,
two chirps, two more than there was supposed to be. Well
fuck, he thought, sounds like Osmond remembered too late
that he wasn't supposed to turn off his alarm so he turned it
back on again. Rudd chuckled at this as he stood in the lot
behind Tony's, chuckled and chuckled more, not so much
because it was funny but because the chuckling felt good, was
a way to relieve the tension and make him forget what was
going on all around him, corpses in the freezer and earshot
executions, chuckle feel like cool air like insideofmycar. So
cool, his eyes shimmered shut, and with his hand he pushed
back his hair. He even swayed a little, back, forth. He heard
the shots, Osmond killing those men, Cash and Cards, but
Rudd didn't know that yet. He jammed the ammo boxes into
his pockets and drew his Walther. The shots came from the
street. The men were in the street. Rudd headed into the
alley. The alley led to the street. He went there, feeling cold,
went out to the street, his balls rising, tight in his Calvins.

Rudd came under fire as he sprang out of the alley and
into the street, but it was unpracticed fire and he wasn't hit.
He skidded onto his side and scrambled back into the alley for
the cover of the corner of Tony's. With no time lost he peeked

back around the corner and acquired his targets, eight or ten men running down the street. Rudd emptied a clip into the small group, dropping at least two men and causing the rest to rethink their advance. This was all Fenton needed, and with wonderful ease he stood to his full height and got off four shots, dropping a man for himself and likely wounding at least one other. As Fenton was firing Miles sprang from his position between cars and ran full-on for the alley where Rudd stood. He fired wildly during the run, his attention being more focused on his destination than on making any significant contribution to the odds, but did manage to hit one man in the arm, and that man's gun flew from his hand and slid under a parked car; he ran off, disarmed and frightened. Miles made the alley unharmed and threw his body against the brick wall next to Rudd. The move looked straight out of a seventies television program like *Starsky and Hutch* or maybe *Baretta*, very practiced though that was unlikely, and Rudd was impressed.

"Shit!" said Miles. "I've only got two and half clips left. My fucking backup ammo was stolen. You should see my car! It's a fucking mess! I'm gonna need Langston's gun."

All the while bullets were striking and chipping the brick corner of their protection, return fire from the assaulting gang, which had taken positions between parked cars and, in one case, a doorway.

"We'll deal with that later," said Rudd. "Right now we've got to get Fenton and Osmond back here and get inside." He paused. He knew what to do, but he felt it best to appear reflective for a moment so that Miles would be less likely to argue with him. "Put a full clip in your Colt."

Miles looked at him but just did it. "Now what," he said when he was finished and waiting for Rudd to reload his Walther.

"Now we step out and fire like hell. Hopefully Fenton and Osmond will use the opportunity to make a break."

Miles held up his hand. "Wait a second. What if they don't? We'll waste all this ammo for nothing."

"So aim at something," Rudd told him. "On three."

And they pivoted out from the corner mellifluously, like two bronze gargoyles on a well-oiled iron gate, their weapons ablaze with anger and caprice, the ebullience of youth, money, and guns.

Rudd almost wanted to laugh, and would have had it not been so inappropriate. He wasn't afraid at all, he realized much to his satisfaction and chagrin. Money he had but money may not mean much in a world where the firing line had moved from the alleys and boom cars out into the streets, and upscale restaurants became fortresses. The mirth of open season took him back to snowball fights and forts; it also reminded him of how far he'd come. He felt old. Miles was doing okay, thought Rudd. Bang bang bang, follow my lead.

Miles was afraid, but it was a hell of a kick. C'mon, fat old Osmond, get your ass over here, he thought of his maladjusted friend, and of himself.

Fenton, certain that Rudd would provide it, had been waiting for this opportunity; such were the benefits to be gleaned by spending too much time in the company of the same man. When it came he was ready. He knew it would take a lot to get Osmond to abandon his cover—mere words wouldn't cut it—so he began by running up to where Osmond crouched and leaving himself fully exposed to the hostile fire. Doing this, Fenton hoped, would give Osmond the illusion that it was somehow okay to step out and run alongside him. Fenton wasn't much of a man, his dad once told him during one of that man's many drunken binges, but he knew a follower when he met one. Bullets whispered about like a restless audience under the drum beat of many many percussions. Fenton stopped next to Osmond and watched a man die under fire from his Glock. It felt bad and good, terrible, horrific. He felt the stirrings of an erection.

"Let's go!" he yelled at Osmond. "Follow me!"

But Fenton waited, knowing that it would be unwise to be between the panicky Osmond and his target. Indeed, Osmond came dashing from his cover, screaming under a burst of fire from his twin forty-fours; serious lead being directed by a less-than-skillful hand (though his earlier performance *had* been rather impressive). These were men building body counts; they had little time for finesse.

Rudd waxed proud when he heard the advance of Fenton and Osmond from behind, heard Osmond's Smiths more than anything. Down the street another man dropped under Rudd's fire, and Rudd hoped it *was* his fire and not some wild shot of Osmond's or Miles's. Fenton's Glock had a distinctive report, and Rudd was happy to see another man take a direct hit from it. Rudd finished off his clip. Miles followed. They fell back around to their cover just as Fenton and Osmond came barreling in behind them. The men stood gasping for air and surveying each other for damage. The group beyond rallied, evidenced by their advancing firepower, and Rudd reached for his own Glock. It occurred to him that he might have favored this gun a moment earlier for its superior clip capacity. But he always preferred the Walther, and now was no time to back away from a quality experience. He was glad that he'd killed his first man with his Walther. The Glock, that was more for maintenance.

"Go! You guys go while I give 'em another blast!" Rudd commanded the others. "It'll only take a second," he added in an effort to preempt any remonstrance, or as a way not to have to be sure that none would be offered.

Fenton nodded and led Miles and Osmond down the alley to the lot behind Tony's. Rudd readied his Glock and fired twice blindly around the corner before stepping out and emptying his clip. He saw one more man fall; then he ran down the alley in the footsteps of his men. In the back Langston stood guarding the door. All this time, he did nothing but listen. Amazing discipline, maximum efficacy.

As soon as he had a clear view of the back lot and saw that it was safe, Fenton yelled, "It's us, Langston!"

"Open the door! Open the door!" screamed Osmond, though the door was plainly open.

Langston had heard them running toward him and hoped that Fenton would think ahead to identify himself. If he hadn't Langston would have been forced to close the door for the protection of Jill and the busboy, though the latter

could probably survive out here better than any of them.
Langston was fully prepared to defend the door to the best of
his abilities. He was certain he could do it, and now he
wouldn't have to. He cleared out of the way as the three men
filed in, brushing past him like so many Kmart shoppers
through a turnstile: Langston could smell it, there would be
coupons presented and discounts taken during the ensuing
days as a result of this excursion.

"Rudd's on his way," Fenton told Langston.

"Good," said Langston, and had he been able to see he
would have appreciated the look that Fenton returned.
Though not friends these men were close.

Rudd came in and the men saw that the door was secure,
and they went back to the bar and resumed drinking and it
felt like they'd never left. Osmond had his vodka martini
and Miles his Cutty Sark; Rudd and Fenton drank J&B,
Langston the Glenlivet. Jill and the busboy did not drink,
but Jill did try to stay involved in the conversation. The
busboy tried to stay in the kitchen. And in truth, he drank
from a jug of red wine he'd found in there, but surreptitiously from a coffee cup.

Rudd was good and drunk and that was good, depending
how one looked at such things, as they all were often drunk
(and good occasionally) men, these seated here in this bar.

"Not bad for a mouse gun!" he roared through the
scotch, Rudd did. "Hey, Miles!"

"What's that you're crowing about?"

"My little mouse gun blew away some major ass out there
this morning."

"Could've done more with a forty-five."

"Like you? Hah!"

"I was short on ammo."

"My point exactly!" exclaimed Rudd, but then his head dropped a notch.

Miles merely grunted, not following but not being in top debating form himself. The thing fizzled out, but Fenton knew how it was: the guys who were into guns tended to have gun mentalities, and all the penis envy that goes with that. That's why the gun magazines editorialized themselves and every guy who ever worked in any gun shop sold himself into stereotype hell with the spurious Kill Power argument. They all were searching for surrogate dicks with big bullets. Nobody would admit that a twenty-two is every bit as lethal as a forty-five. Fenton thought about the weight lifters at his gym, how they'd all apparently made some secret unspoken agreement about wearing the big leather belts all the time, whether lifting or not. As long as we all do this all the time then everybody will think we have a good reason.

"What about that plastic piece of shit?" demanded Miles out of nowhere, but evidently conceding the first point.

Before Rudd could rise to response he was preempted by Fenton, who said quite gravely, "Polymer, Miles. The Glocks we carry have a polymer frame. Not plastic."

Everybody respected this of course. That point was won. And way.

"Yeah, well at least yours has some bite to it. A forty you could carry with pride. Hell, I'd carry a forty if I had to. Forty's not a nine," grumbled Miles, looping back.

A lull ensued. This kind of contentious crap wasn't the best part of drinking, but it had to be got through like all the rest.

"I need a gun," said Jill. "Maybe Langston's if he's done with it. If not, then one of Rudd's or Osmond's. Those guys have two. I need one."

She held her ground. Rudd thought it was cute but tried to stop thinking it when his addled brain reminded him that she probably wouldn't appreciate the characterization. Cute.

Miles looked ugly and tossed off, "Sorry, sweetie. I'll be needing Langston's gun. *And* his ammo." This last while looking at Rudd, who did not notice.

"I'm taking Langston's ammo for my Glock," said Rudd. "You use your forty-five conservatively till you're out. Then we'll decide what to do from there. It may not even come to that." Cute: I need a gun.

"All except for one clip," said Langston.

Rudd thought he was passed out, and the boom of his regal voice startled him. "Of course," he said, "you'll keep a clip in your Beretta, Langston."

"Yes," pronounced Langston. "And I'll give my Beretta to Jill."

"You're fucking kidding me!" wailed Miles.

But his voice betrayed defeat. Miles couldn't possibly win this, not after what happened that morning. Rudd had taken the morning; there could be little question of that. Nobody spoke. Langston knew he wouldn't be challenged by anyone but Rudd, and Rudd wouldn't challenge him at all.

"I get to keep my guns?" asked Osmond. "Both of them?"

"They're yours," Rudd declared, playing something of the spin doctor here. "You do what you want with them; that's the point. Langston does what he wants with his Beretta. He can give it to the busboy if he wants."

In the kitchen the busboy's ears pricked up at the sound of this, but he wasn't really listening anyway and he folded back to his wine. Langston unloaded his Beretta and field stripped it with quick facile fingers unhampered by his eyes. This man no longer required a gun anymore than he craved a target.

"Come here, Jill," he said. "I'll get you comfortable with this thing and then we can squeeze off a round or two for practice."

"Now we're doing target practice?" said Miles as he stared into his drink. "What's next, mixology school?"

The men all froze at the implication. There was a finite amount of liquor in this place just as surely as there were only so many bullets. A day might come when there would be no more liquor here and still be men.

Jill stood. "Better two or three now than have me screw up later when it counts," she said to everyone present, but mostly to herself and Miles. She crossed to Langston, sat down next to him.

Rudd said, "That's right, we only have so much booze. Where is it, Jill? Is it downstairs?"

Already she was absorbed in the Beretta, which Langston had handed to her reassembled a moment before becoming himself absorbed in the new question at hand. "Yeah," she said. She fingered the gun. It was an amazing thing, the stuff

legends were made of. "I'll show you later." It was foreboding
too, disgusting really, gross. It really is like a penis, she
reflected, a hard ugly dick and now I've got to fuck it because
I've come this far and I'm here and it's the only way to keep
face with these men.

Exasperated, Rudd looked around for the busboy. The
kitchen, as usual, he thought. Probably in there drinking the
last of the J&B.

"Where's the liquor, Jill? Where's the rest of it? Where's
all of it?" Langston demanded gently but no question: he
wanted an answer now.

She looked up from the gun, hurt. Somehow she'd expected a continuing alliance with this man. She should have
known better—she did really. There were certain topics you
didn't fuck with them over. This one especially. Booze. This
one with these men. No, I won't show you, you fucker, she
thought. But she had the gun; it was hers now. That was
something. "Do I take you down or Rudd?"

"We all go," said Miles, standing.

Jill shrugged, gripped the gun, and wondered about the
holster, was it part of the bargain. "It'll be crowded," she
warned. Didn't matter: holster or no, she could and would
carry it. It was hers now.

The rest of them rose and Jill led the way to dry-storage,
holding the gun with her hand wrapped completely around
the barrel and trigger guard. When they reached the top of
the stairs she merely gestured them down. They filed past her
and she stepped over to the kitchen and looked in on the
busboy. He was drinking from a coffee cup, she saw. He saw

the gun in her hand but did not react. They exchanged a glance that was awkward at best, neither one of them having any idea what their relationship should be but suspecting that there was something that bound them separate from the men. But then there were other things, maybe stronger things, that bound Jill to the men and excluded the busboy, he thought. White things. Jill turned and walked back to the bar to wait for the men with their questions. That busboy, probably just another swinging dick at heart, she thought.

In time and after much inspection the men returned to the bar, clustered about. Grumbling and bumping, perhaps pausing in their assertive shuffles, they eventually considered their seats and betook there their rumps.

"So maybe thirty days, right?" opined Fenton.

Some of the men snorted a laugh, but Fenton wasn't sure who except that it wasn't Rudd. He felt foolish and new at this, still: simple math . . .

"If we're careful," said Rudd, feeling protective.

"Bullshit," declared Miles.

"I'd say that's pretty optimistic." Langston.

Osmond: "Bullshit!"

Fenton was wounded. He didn't care about any of this. He felt his hand tremble, but maybe not. It occurred to him how much he wanted a drink right at that moment, as in craving. Sympathy pains, he thought, looking at Rudd. Thirty days, bullshit.

Rudd exhaled heavily the heat and worry of his lungs. He turned and watched Langston, blind man, smell the liquor through the bottles, wise enough to count and enough of a drunk to be afraid like they all were. Work expands to fill the time allotted it, something like that his dad said now and again. There would be a corollary that would apply here, he guessed. But he said,

"This is how it will be: Everybody will share equal responsibility for our supply of liquor. Nothing comes out of the storage room without it being approved by, well, all of us, I guess, or a vote or my order or something. We can work that out; point is that nobody—absolutely nobody, not even me—ever removes a bottle from that room by himself, that is to say with only his own knowledge. Okay, wait, I'm getting off the track. I want the supply guarded twenty-four hours a day. I'm fairly certain it's secure against outside penetration, but we all know how it might get in here. We're all in the same boat as far as that goes, all except for Jill and the kid in there. I think they should stand guard duty just the same though. Everybody must take a turn at this most important post. Let's face it: that liquor is why we came here and it's why we're staying here . . . well, the riot too. Everybody pulls a shift alone. If a man is made solely responsible for something at a given time I think it's the best way to give him a stake in things, to keep him honest. I'm not accusing anybody or even suggesting that one of us might steal from the others. But the temptation might be great at times, physically necessary at times. We'll always deal with that of course. As a group. Point is to seek the higher ground. I truly believe this. Each man spends time alone with the bottles, his responsibility. The higher moral ground."

Day5

I'm talking about those moments when it becomes clear that a certain new aspect—bad or good—of our life has been accepted by the world at large." Rudd waxed philosophical over his brandy, his eyes full of arousal, thoughts of his life and what made him good. "I'm talking about the moment of cultural assimilation."

Jill, seated across from him in the booth, watched as he topped off their glasses. Though she'd hardly touched hers, she was trying to keep a pace of sorts. She wanted to be interested in what he was saying, if for no other reason than to fill the oppressive void of watching them all passed out. "I think I know what you're saying," she said.

He nodded, anxious to be in receipt of this, her volley. "Let me give you two examples," he said, mellow yet almost out of breath.

Langston dozed on the benches near the front, a fixture now. He dreamed of small girls, men's daughters.

Osmond, Fenton, and Miles were engaged in conversation at the bar. The latter two kept glancing at Jill and Rudd.

Rudd wore that look on his face, like Bear with me, you'll get it. "I needed a bandanna—I know, I know: it was for a party, I was going to a sixties party—so I went into one of those kids' stores—skates and records, stuff like that—and they had them. The woman asked me what color I wanted, and she held out a red one. She looked at me, presumably waiting to see if I wanted red." He paused to make sure this had all sunk in, that the significance of a red bandanna was not lost on Jill.

"I don't think I could see you in a red bandanna," said Jill. No help.

"Well obviously," Rudd continued, straightforward, best plan, "that's why I said to her 'Jeez, not red! I wear that and I'll get shot.' 'Does that still happen?' she said, laughing. And that was it. It was significant because it was such a casual joke. The idea of being shot for wearing the wrong color scarf had become nothing more than a joke. No more: oh yeah, isn't that awful, or: oh, I know what you mean. It had fulfilled its destiny. It had to become a joke because there was simply no other way to deal with it, no other way to challenge its power."

Jill was nodding, she was close. "I'm with you," she said. She was tipsy, thank God.

"Right, right," said Rudd. He choked down a gulp of brandy. " 'Nother example, this time a good one. Walking down the street on a sunny Sunday afternoon, just me out for a walk. Semi-residential neighborhood, a few liquor stores and banks, maybe a grocery store . . ." He paused, momentarily lost. Too much detail, he thought. But that's the best way, right? Rudd sipped his brandy. "I'm walking, and this car pulled up—a BMW I think, one of those kids' ones, 320 something. In fact it was full of kids, young women, I should say. The driver, about twenty-five, attractive blond, leaned over her friend and said to me, 'Do you know if there's a Plus machine nearby?' Not an ATM, she didn't ask for an ATM. She asked for a Plus machine! She asked a total stranger for a Plus machine, and the best part is: I knew exactly what she meant and where one was. I told her, and she thanked me and drove off. Beautiful, I thought. ATMs are now assimilated, so much so that we need to be more specific when discussing them—"

He was interrupted by Miles, who brazenly wedged his way into their conversation, into the booth and next to Jill. "What are we talking about?" he wanted to know.

Ignoring him, or at least resolved to attempt so, Rudd concluded directly to Jill, "Like the colored bandannas, the Plus machines are now a piece of history. We don't have to ask about them anymore, it's not a question. It's a—"

"What's a plus machine?" asked Miles of Jill.

She looked to Rudd. She had been nodding too vigorously and now she needed him to answer quick.

"Do you *mind*, Miles?" challenged Rudd, turning on the man.

She felt she had to jump in with something. "We were talking about how people communicate," she said.

"Thank you, Jill," said Rudd, looking at Miles as if declared the victor by the ranking authority. He turned to Jill. "—fact," he said. "Knowledge. It's knowledge."

"Eggheads," said Miles dismissively, before passing out on the table.

Rudd assessed the situation. "You're trapped," he said.

Later, standing alone in the restroom, she examined her naked body in the mirror as she bathed. She had rigged up something of a hand shower using some hose from the maintenance closet and taking advantage of the floor drain in the ladies' room. It was clear, if unspoken, to Jill and all the men that this was her private domain, this room. No one but her entered ever. The men bathed in the kitchen, at the dishwashing sink, when they bathed at all, and of course they had the men's room.

She had been secretly washing her undergarments, twice now, letting them dry in here. She'd walked about, those two times, secretly not wearing underwear and fearing the connotation that such an act might hold for these men. A statement. Knowledge, Rudd would call it, a fact. She wondered if this no-underwear thing that men seemed to have would qualify as a cultural assimilation under his rules. On both occasions she ended up feeling, well, *observed*, before her bra and panties were dry; she had gone back to the ladies' room, utilized the hot air from the electric hand dryer.

What's the big deal, she wondered, wiping her breasts with a wet paper towel. Plenty of paper towels these days, like a mini post-nuclear movie, all the stuff you want. Jill saw a movie once on cable, *The World, the Flesh, and the Devil*. Harry Belafonte is left alone on planet earth with a white woman, no problem until a white guy shows up. One scene has this woman throwing dirty dishes out of her high-rise kitchen window rather than wash them. Someday when the pile gets too high I'll have to move, the woman muses, or so Jill remembers it. It's really the only scene she remembers from the movie, that one and the beginning where Harry is trapped in a mine and banging a rock and singing. Harry (Henry?) was only modestly black at best—probably the only way to sell the public on the potential romance with the white chick at the time—but that chick was pure as the driven snow. She could afford to throw a lot of dishes out that window before she'd even have to start looking, let alone moving.

Jill was utterly confused. She'd been here before, a few times. Her first weeks in college was one time, first weeks as a woman another. Maybe before that even. Maybe after. Call it more than a few times.

If she slept with only one of the men that would be too much of a statement. If she slept with all of them it might be worse. She was a woman and she wasn't allowed any slack; if she had sex with one of these men the act would be indelible, just as if one of them had sex with another of them. She didn't know, wasn't sure. Maybe the world was different; the outside world certainly was. Still, best play it safe and fuck somebody. At least one. Nothing's that different, she thought. And there was the wash rag and she did sort of an impromptu breast examination, which was sort of funny. But okay too.

Rudd was on duty down in dry-storage. He had just returned after a short trip upstairs to mix himself a new drink in the presence of the others. That was part of the agreement, or at least the spirit, of guarding dry-storage: you never touched the liquor. If you wanted a drink you went up to the bar and got one. Rudd sipped carefully. He was an honorable man, and holding to the letter of the law was more important than the thought of somebody—Miles, almost certainly—

slipping down a gulp of this or that while down here alone. It frightened Rudd, this integrity. It frightened him because it threatened to be the first thing in his life that could conceivably take precedence over alcohol. He really *wouldn't* pilfer a sip of scotch merely to equal the suspected consumption of a lesser man.

He swirled the ice in his rocks glass. He *would* kill another man to protect his supply. Had in fact, perhaps. That made him smile. The ice in his glass made him smile too, bathed in scotch as it was. Rudd could look into this glass (something Langston could no longer do, it occurred) and see his own distorted reflection, all bumped and fucked up by ice and booze. So many years and so many drinks, most of them alone like this one, and never had he had such a clear picture of himself, distorted though it was. Things were getting better. Gunfire and explosions punctuated the night, getting worse all the time. Things would never be all right again, but they were better.

He would sleep with her. He knew that now, sitting amidst his—the—bottles. And for the silliest of reasons, the most truly unbelievable of reasons: he would sleep with her—rather she would sleep with him—because she liked him. Maybe even she liked him a lot. It didn't matter. Any way you cut it she liked him and felt safe with him and wanted to fuck him. And it wouldn't be all that long now either. It would be soon. He thought about that other waitress in that other dry-storage so many years ago. That Gail; he remembered her when he first walked into this place two days ago, remembered fleetingly, one might say. Now the important thing to consider was that that event, that Gail some twenty-plus years ago, that was a loss. That was a boy with his dad's withered dick talking, and damn softly at that. This girl, this Jill, this will be a win, a victory, and not in any puerile locker-room schoolboy way. No, Jill will give him power over not only the other men but himself as well. For the first time in his life Rudd will win. Fuck you again, Dad.

He turned up his glass to empty it of scotch and one of the ice cubes hit him in the nose. That made him laugh because he remembers being at cocktail parties and using that tiny event as a barometer to limit his drinking, an early warning sign of sorts. That was a different life, gone forever. Nothing from that life would ever matter again. That Gail might be dead, killed in the riots. An ice cube hits your nose now and it's time for more scotch. But slow down just the same. There's work to be done. Rudd got an erection and thought about jerking off and decided not to for the same reason that he decided not to refill his drink just yet. Thing about women, he thought, they have pussies. Then he laughed.

Jill stepped from the ladies' room after a lengthy session with the mirror that left her feeling tousled and worn down. They made you do this, act this way. The fuckers really *did* make woman in their own image, or from their rib, whatever.

The men in the bar looked up as one when she turned the corner into the room. They didn't know this of course, but she saw it, saw it like they were so many marionettes, their heads bobbing up from a pull on their strings. Bob bob, bounce, back to the drinks, maybe a smile or stupid grin, a leer. No two marionettes are created equal. They're like snowflakes, she knew.

"Rudd downstairs?" she asked. Okay, now they knew too, the snowflakes.

Miles and Osmond glanced at each other. God! the things she knew about them, these men. Things the fuckers had no clue about. These guys were just big kids building snowmen out of snowflakes. Or taking them from their ribs.

"Come keep me company, my dear," lilted Langston from the front of the room. "I'm a drunk and now I'm blind, and I suppose I'm old too."

He sat up, but she could see only the top of his head from behind the bar.

"Hell of an offer, no?" he continued. "How's the Beretta?"

She fingered the outline of the gun jammed into her pocket. This was how she preferred to carry it though the men had offered other options. Maybe that was why she carried it like this: it pissed them off. "I can field strip it faster than you, I bet. Got it down cold."

"Sorry to hear that," said Langston. "I was hoping you were just glad to see me."

The men all giggled. Some of them snickered and others tittered.

Jill didn't even crack a smile. "Let's start a pool on what joke gets told the most during our time together here," she said. "I've got dibs on that square." She turned toward the stairs.

"You'll find him down there," volunteered Fenton, who alone felt sympathy for her, at least at that moment.

She paused at the top of the stairs and turned back to have a look at Fenton. There was a beat of decision for effect, the kind you supply when the decision has already been made, before she walked over to where the man sat alone on the long side of the bar. Everybody watched this but nobody looked, except for Fenton, who did her the courtesy of turning to face her approach. These were two people now. It was one of those special moments, like a flavored coffee commercial only real.

"I need to ask you a favor," she said to him, very close, bowing her head to his ear and knowing that he would remain motionless as she did so. This was not an opportunistic man. "I need to ask you something."

He nodded slightly, vertically. "Of course," he said.

None of the men could hear any of this and it made them feel fucked in a backhanded way. Masturbating with your left hand.

She whispered, "I need to be undisturbed, downstairs I mean."

He whispered, "You shall be." And then he said, "Understood," before returning to his drink. A tribute of sorts, both these things.

Rudd found himself growing impatient by the time he heard Jill padding down the steps, and it was only then that it occurred to him that he had no concrete reason to expect her at all, no reason period, at least not then, not enough reason to be sucking ice cubes.

But then these thoughts may have had more to do with an empty glass than with the situation, and when she arrived in dry-storage Jill found Rudd fully prepared for her arrival. Her ego, reasonably yet inexplicably, was bruised.

"What a nice surprise," he said.

She swallowed this. Okay, she thought, we're through that.

"I guess I'm out of scotch." He held up his drink, then retracted it quickly lest she mistake this for a request when really he was just trying to think of something to say. A drink would be nice though.

"Maybe you won't need it," she said, tossing her hair gently, hoping for an effect of some sort. She decided to go with it, and that thing about lie back and enjoy it flitted through her head then was gone. She wondered why. The stairs were behind her. She had legs. There was an impulse (there would be). She bit it back and wondered how that looked to men—to Rudd—when she tossed her hair like that.

Rudd felt a twinge of panic. This was real; you never believed it until . . . well, until you believed it. Suddenly it all seemed much bigger than an erection, and that worried him and the thought that he was worried worried him because he knew all too well where that could lead. Then he remembered he was fairly drunk and was able to relax. "Come sit," he said, moving his chair as close as he dared to the other one that had been placed down here. Stupid, he thought, that looked stupid, I should have pulled over the empty one. Too leading?

I don't have time to come sit, she thought, realizing that there was the whole problem: she could—perhaps would—sit forever. Why did she need this? Why. She did, she always did. Good Lord, she thought, what if I can't make it happen? What then?

She couldn't think about that now; she couldn't afford to. She ignored the chair, trying hard to make that itself into a gesture, and with surprising (and reassuring) grace straddled Rudd's lap and lowered herself onto him for what should now be a kiss. C'mon, she thought, you know how to do this.

Snap to! he thought, and wondered what to do with his glass. This stuff *never* goes smoothly for him. He hoped it was that way for everyone. Can't just drop it; it would shatter and that would break the mood. Rudd realized that Jill knew what she was doing, kept up the motion, one fluid move from the time she walked toward him to this moment, her lips heading for his. He held the glass, doing his best to hug her with it in his hand, and received her kiss. Now make her feel that erection.

"Just a second," he said, pulling away when he deemed the kiss confirmed. He turned and placed the glass on the shelf behind him, keeping her braced with one arm. A strong arm.

Then he took her fully, the two of them necking in the one chair there like a couple of teenagers. If you could forget everything for a moment, if you could pretend that this was supposed to happen, well then it felt pretty good.

Awkwardly, yet still a good movie move, Rudd stood from the chair, lifting Jill along with him and pressing her into an alcove formed by an absence of liquor shelving against the far wall and in the right corner. It wasn't so bad and she said,

"Wait a minute."

He backed off long enough to let her unsnap and pull down her pants, panties going right along because she figured it would give him less chance to screw up a so-far-so-good performance if she did it for him. There she stood, self-satisfied at being able to achieve a wetness in herself and an erection in him. Having been through this scene a godvillion times she knew now that it was time to wait for his hand between her legs, his can-only-hope-they're-clean fingers to penetrate her like some sort of advance scout for his penis.

Time to touch her,

thought Rudd, and he was pleased to find her wet, waiting and willing to receive his touch, is what that was supposed to mean. Of course just before–during?–being pleased he felt that instant of shock, like this is *reality*, and it made him want to pull away, want to scream out something like: Whoa! Wait a minute! I didn't think it would be like *this*. She parted and he pushed a middle finger tentatively into her which cued her to part further which cued him to push a second finger in. Some short minutes were spent here, and the kisses were ongoing and nice. Then acceleration took over, or maybe it was anticipation or maybe merely knowing the play, but he said,

"Okay,"

absurdly like it was his place to say such a thing, and then he pulled down his own pants, which snagged on his erect penis and hurt him momentarily so that when he took down his underwear he wondered about guys in porn movies and the abuse their penises seemed to take, wondered if he was overly sensitive down there, or overly sensitive in general. Compared to a guy in a porn movie, that is.

Jill took this opportunity to remove her pants totally from her feet, though one pant leg remained pulled to constriction around her right foot. Still the access was there now, and she figured the dangling pant leg wouldn't mean much in the grand scheme of things. Right away, when he lifted her by the buttocks and inserted himself into her

rather skillfully, he thought, like those insensitive guys in the porn movies (was he insensitive?)

she knew she was wrong. Wrong about the pant leg. Her feet were airborne and that otherwise weightless piece of cloth was pulling at her ankle like some fucking insane cotton conscience. He didn't hurt; in fact he felt okay, pretty good even, if you wanted to get optimistic about it, yet all she could think about was that pant leg dangling there, twisting her ankle. She'd never walk again. And the worst part: the men wouldn't care. She sort of tried to shove it off with her other foot, but her heart wasn't in it because after all what could your foot do that your hand can't? Run?

He probably thinks this is how I move, she thought.

"I got it," he said apprehensively.

Reaching back with one hand while effortlessly supporting her with the other, he deftly shucked it from her foot, utterly flustering her. They resumed their rhythm, and Jill was so close to coming when Rudd finally ejaculated that she had to award him the point anyway. He did get it. A technical thing. A percentile thing.

There was this afterthought that snapped like a stretched rubber behind her eyes in front of the mirror of the ladies' room as she later wiped the residue of Rudd from between her legs with a paper towel. It always came down to this, her alone with herself and a mirror and a bunch of goo and the feeling that if she'd tried a little harder then everything wouldn't seem so empty at this moment. This was a day. These fucking lives we lead, they always even out, rear their little heads no matter how fucked up the outside world got. Like being homeless, what about being homeless? Does anything really change besides the scenery? She thought about masturbating but that really *would* be maudlin, the perfect cap to solitude. Best to mitigate the blame, was the specious presumption under which she had always operated. Rudd remained down in dry-storage. Jill headed out to be with the other drunks, the men at the bar.

It was pretty smooth, stepping out there. She knew it would be. She felt empowered and they were all docile, considered her enough of a person to not say anything hostile or untoward. They were all drunk and she was so afraid of that damn *bath*room she kept retreating to. What would they say? What could they say if things were terrible? She couldn't begin to fathom the possibilities. Did they even want her around? Would Rudd speak to her again? Did he think he owned her, the stupid lumbering fuck. After all he wasn't her father.

She smiled at Fenton, also at Langston because why not? But she sauntered over to where Miles and Osmond sat next to each other at the bar. "I'm ready for a drink," she said, music-video saucy and her Self positioned in the space between them, a step back but insistent like: let me in.

Osmond was a deer in the lights; no surprise there. Miles lifted his ass and hopped down a seat, parting the sea.

"Join us," he said, smiling. Most of the right moves for all of the wrong reasons.

Now that's what I call tonic, she thought. "Maybe something sweet?" she ventured, looking at Osmond demurely as a way to look at Miles. Fenton was watching her, Langston listening. Good, she thought.

She felt Miles rise behind her, held Osmond's gaze momentarily before turning to his touch on her shoulder.

"I've got just the thing," he said as he slipped behind the bar.

She knew it would be a one hundred proof something that looked and tasted like Kool-Aid. Good again, that's what she was here for. She thought briefly about the busboy, but what would be the point. Osmond put his hand on her leg and said something to her. She responded. He gurgled something back, and she could tell he thought he'd succeeded at being witty, maybe even charming. Well he had; this was success. Osmond grew bolder with Miles's return and replaced the hand on her leg with his other hand then moved the former to her back. He did it without ever completely losing contact with her as if she might run away or was a hologram that he'd managed to touch and was waiting for his friends to take over touch patrol while he alerted the proper scientific authorities. She sucked down her drink and looked at the empty glass and laughed at something Miles said as he went to fetch another. She awaited the proper authorities. Slipping softly now Jill was but still fingers on the ledge like the twenty fingers on her body what with two men and two hands each moving from tentative placement on her back and thighs to aggressive probing. Their boldness grew exponentially. Each failure of No meant a louder Yes. She knew that. If these guys had any guts they'd cut out her liver with a butter knife, but she knew that the most she could hope for would be a slap or two from Miles. Then she could go back to the ladies' room and be alone. She slipped into autopilot and settled back to watch the show.

Then it was as late as it gets in a day, and Jill sat, not in the ladies' room where she had envisioned herself, but in the kitchen. Vacantly she tore strips of chicken off a carcass that had been removed from the freezer by the busboy the night before. The men didn't eat much, so the kid had been forced to forage for himself. This was no problem, of course, once he got used to averting his eyes from the unnatural shape of the bartender in the back of the freezer. Jill wasn't thinking about that or even the chicken. A tear was latched in the corner of one eye, refusing to break loose, and she was damned if she'd help things along, pull the finger from the dike. The busboy, fed up with chicken yet resenting Jill's participation in the spoils, sat impassively reading an old *People* magazine in the very far corner of the kitchen. He wanted to look scary. He was beginning to suspect that his role here was yet to be revealed. He wanted to be a virus.

Jill was fucked. Fenton and Langston seemed unlikely though it hardly mattered now, and the busboy wasn't even in play. Her head pounded. She was nauseated. It wasn't until she noticed, in her peripheral vision, the kid lift his head to look at her (her thinking Okay, fucker, you got something to say, say it! something to ask for, just try to ask) that she heard the yelling from just outside the back door. Heard it maybe, but didn't differentiate it from the usual sounds of violence beyond that terrible door until the kid looked up at her and she saw the question that really was in his face: What you gonna do with that?

Carey had seen the smoke rising from the ventilation system the night before, but nobody had emerged since then and he wasn't sure what he was getting into banging on the door like this. They had to be white, he knew, and he hated to think that that was the reason he was trying to get in. But it was.

"Hello! I really need to get in!"

Carey remembers swearing once before a group of people that he would never enter a bastion of Republicanism such as Tony's, would in fact sooner die. Maybe they wouldn't answer. Would he? He was making too much noise, but there weren't a lot of other options. He couldn't face another night in the laundry room of his apartment building, couldn't go upstairs 'cause it was charred rubble. He never should have stayed— he was totally surrounded now in never-never land—but he couldn't come to terms with running, hiding in some shelter behind a phalanx of Blue. The Man. One look at the Guardsman lowering the concrete barricades into place around the YMCA and Carey's skin began to crawl. The Revolution had come, just as he and his friends had predicted during endless nights of discussion and espresso, but it turned into nothing more than a bunch of recklessly armed opportunistic assholes carrying VCRs under their arms and mugging for scared-shitless TV news crews shooting from INside their remote vans. Latter-day Trojans, those news crews, going nowhere fast. He'd seen one of those vans overturned and heard the screams from inside as the mob fell upon the doors and windows. The first black eye he met after that told him You're in the wrong place. Well, be careful what you wish for.

Jill knew this was a white guy in trouble. She couldn't make out exactly what he was saying through the door, but the intent was clear: save my white ass. The busboy, when he saw in her face that she would open the door, disgustedly drifted back to his *People*. Jill got up and started working the locks, thinking, do this before one of them stops me. The Beretta, still tucked in her pocket was more something to be possessed than used. She realized this when she failed to pull it out even though she remembered it was there and the time would be now. But then there were plenty of reasons to be opening the door. These guns, the thing men didn't get about them, you take it all on a case-by-case basis. Use it now, maybe not later. Depends. A man, you hand him a gun and his finger falls right into position on the trigger.

Carey heard the locks turning and prepared himself for his fate. When the door finally whooshed open and he stood face-to-face with Jill he was caught completely off guard. A white woman was probably the closest thing to a safe minority right now. A best-case scenario for a man who couldn't make up his mind whether he was looking to bunk with Rodney King or Daryl Gates.

Why is this guy still alive, was Jill's first thought upon seeing the man before her. He was frail and afraid with thin dark hair and wire-framed glasses. She wondered what kind of gun he carried.

"I saw smoke from the ventilator last night," he started in, wanting to say a lot in a short amount of time, to justify his knock.

"That was chicken cooking," she said. Well it was. She looked past him into the night. Scattered fires glowed against the clouds, the dome of the city. "You'd better come in."

Rather than step away she tugged on his arm, and he willingly followed her lead. When they were both inside Jill closed the door and both of them fell upon the locks, he working as if he'd just returned home.

I'm locking myself inside Tony's, he thought.

Langston, who had heard and dismissed the opening door, was certain now that something was up in the kitchen. Miles and Osmond were technically passed out in a booth and Rudd was still in dry-storage.

"Fenton," he said, instinctively reaching for and not finding his Beretta.

"I got it," said Fenton, wondering if he should alert Rudd after spending all this time being grateful that his friend was downstairs and missing the unseemly bulk of this evening's activities. No time, he decided. He drew his Glock and moved silently to the kitchen.

By the time he got there he was certain the locks were being worked and he prepared to spring around the corner with his gun leveled at approximate chest height. For an insane moment he wanted to yell *Freeze!* like some deranged omnipotent TV cop, but he knew it was probably just Jill slipping away into the night, departing this nightmare for another, more anonymous one. He stepped into the kitchen, ready to lock the door behind her, his Glock held half-heartedly away from his thigh.

The bolts all safely thrown, Carey and Jill turned to assess each other.

"I'm Carey," he said extending his hand, thinking, She's pretty, thinking, It's not her fault.

"I'm Jill." She took his hand, shaking it almost gleefully, thinking, He's sober.

"Fenton," said Fenton, who had been observing this unexpected arrival and now crossed the room with his hand extended, forgetting about the Glock.

Carey, who had become more than a little gun-shy during the preceding week, zeroed in on Fenton's readied automatic. "Jesus don't shoot!" he screamed, throwing his back against the door. "Jesus can't you see I'm white!" he said. Jesus, he thought. Shoot. Shoot now.

Day 7

Rudd regretted, as he watched the channel-span of Emergency Broadcast *Stay Tuned* screens with underscoring sound loop, that he had turned off the television the night before. The spotty in-studio rumor reports of nationwide mayhem had gotten to him, and when home video of a concentration-camp–style holding pen on the Las Vegas strip was cued up he simply couldn't take it anymore and snapped off the power, aiming the remote and thinking *bang*. Osmond, who had been fairly engrossed in the report, looked hurt but said nothing in response to Rudd's challenging stare. Well he'd better keep his mouth shut, thought Rudd, Miles too. Fucking rapists. Once in college, as a kid, Rudd had made some moves on a drunk girl who was passed out. Rudd was drunk too, and the girl moaned harshly and brushed him off long before anything really happened. Innocent by fact, he had later wondered how far he would have gone with that girl, but stopped wondering when he couldn't come up with an answer, or even a rationalization, that he liked. That was a drunk kid; Miles and Osmond were grown men. But then Jill, drunk or sober, was of the age of consent as well, and though he didn't know the details of what went down Rudd was pretty sure that she was complicitous in the wrong that was done.

Rudd shut off the television, then thought better of it and turned it back on but with the sound muted. How bad can it get before the army takes over? There were, last night, reports of desertions and he had figured: blacks. But guys run home to protect their families—he would if he had one—maybe leaving only hoary generals with fingers hovering menacingly over buttons and re-calibrated targets, wondering, What should I do? He turned his attention to this Carey. The guy was sitting alone in a booth, writing in a spiral notebook he'd found in the back, sipping a diet soda from an otherwise perfectly good beer mug. A journal, Rudd had said under his breath, derisively to Fenton as they watched the man writing yesterday, and indeed he had later heard the guy tell Jill that he always kept a journal. Jill seemed fascinated by him, and even now she watched him from another booth, waiting for a chance to go and sit across from him and resume what had become some sort of perverse intellectual marathon soul-searching apocalyptic conversation. Rudd watched Jill watch Carey. He was, in short, disgusted.

Well fuck this. He poured himself a too strong drink and, trying hard to ignore the demanding *Stay Tuned*, walked aggressively to Carey's booth. He felt a modicum of gratification as he saw in his peripheral vision what must have been a disapproving look from Jill. He also felt pressure to do well, to upstage this guy. Stay Tuned.

"How's it going there, Carey?"

Carey looked up. He seemed frightened. He seemed resentful.

"It's a journal, right? You're keeping a journal?" Rudd suddenly wanted to be chummy, might be the best shot at impressing Jill. He took the opposite seat, grinning, "Future history, right? Ever see that movie, *War of the Worlds*? The guy's talking into a tape—I think it's a tape, he's a reporter but things are so bad that there's no more station to broadcast from—talking on tape and he says he's doing it for future history, if there is any."

Carey put down his pen. His journal *was* sort of like that scene. "Yeah, I saw it. Then the other guy, the scientist—was it Gene Barry?—he overhears and says something about it to the woman." He was swept up in the recollection, and his face softened wistfully. Carey loved it when fiction touched reality, or more precisely, presaged it. "Now all we need is for the bad guys to catch colds and die." But as he said this his face darkened slightly, though Rudd was nodding in agreement. "I don't really mean that of course." Tony's. He wondered if this place itself harbored some kind of virus, something left over from the Reagan years that shifted people who came here to the right. It would be like that *Star Trek* with the bad space, "The Tholian Web," was it? Always as a kid, he and his brothers, even his dad, watched all the *Star Trek* reruns.

"No, you're right," said Rudd. "That would be great, have them all drop dead in mid sneeze." He sensed that Carey wasn't with him and felt it was time for a declaration. After all, the only way to do any of this was to stand up straight. That's why he was Rudd. That's why he was in charge.

"At least that way I wouldn't have to shoot any more of the motherfuckers," he said and he swallowed deeply of his scotch.

Carey wasn't sure how to take this. He wanted it to be a joke, but he'd heard enough tantamount references during the short time he'd been here to believe that it was probably true. Rudd probably was a murderer; probably all of them were. All these guns. What were they doing with these guns? It was as if they'd been waiting for something like this to happen. *The Hunt*, some bad TV movie from his youth. Carey was tempted to ask Rudd if he remembered it, but he was nothing like this man. Rudd, murderers, all of them. Not Jill though, he was sure.

"Trouble on the television, I guess," he said, pointing.

Rudd winced. Lefty was ducking the subject: no surprise here. "Yeah, looks like they're taking a break. Nap or something. Off the air for a while."

"I'd say it's a little worse than that," said Carey, falling into lecture mode on his face, like he was sitting in some coffee house chastising some poor media pawn on how to listen to what the network news *didn't* report more carefully than to what it did. But it wasn't so bad, maybe this murderer could stand a lecture. "That shit doesn't go on screen unless things are really grim." He liked the sound of that, and it appeared to make the murderer a little edgy. Carey sat back, self-satisfied, and folded his arms. So much for bad space.

Catch this monkey, thought Rudd as he stifled a laugh with his glass. "Nah," he swiped the air dismissively. "What it is is a military order, something like that. Stop the spread of information while they regain control." Be back on the golf course next week, he almost added. Well maybe.

"What, the Guard?" said Carey. "Hey, man, I've been out there. I'm telling you, you see Guard transports deserted, burned, overturned. Three blocks over on Carrington there's a dead Guardsman lying in the middle of the street. Naked." He could feel his language change. At first he'd intended to tone it down a bit and try to blend—this was Tony's—but now he was ready to roll with it, ready to piss these dinosaurs off. Carey began work on some damage control. Maybe he did serve a purpose here after all. "It's not like that anymore, man. There's no army out there. And even if there were, there are no targets, nothing you can drop a bomb on or fire a missile at. Don't you guys watch TV in here—I mean didn't you when it was on? The fucking White House is the Black House."

Rudd felt a jolt of laughter, said, "How did you know—"

"I'm not fucking joking! It's painted right across the front: *Black House*. It was one of the first things to go, a mob materialized and stormed the gates before the Marines knew what hit 'em. They said it was something like twenty thousand people, most of them armed. An irresistible force!" He looked around. Really going now, talking fast, he could keep a room silent for hours when he got like this, had. "Coffee, is there any coffee made?" He spotted Jill, almost asked her for some but didn't want to lose his momentum. Be nice to find a worthy opponent, but not here, not likely. "The president was out, they said. They also said that nobody ever saw the mob coming, but let me ask you: That mob had been coming for years, how could they not have seen it?"

Rudd looked at the man transformed, waiting for him to respond. Okay, Lefty, but one step at a time. "How did you know that he was a Guardsman? If he was naked, how do you know? That's what I was gonna ask before the lecture came down." It occurred to him that he was getting pretty drunk, but his glass was empty now. "Jill, could I trouble you," he said, holding up his glass, having grave doubts about whether this was a good play. The Black House, he thought. What a load of shit.

"And coffee. I need some coffee," bellowed Carey, startling Rudd and forgetting where he was, whom he was with.

After a beat spent with her lip curled up to make it clear that this was a one-time favor, Jill padded off to get the drinks. "I'll have to make some coffee," she said over her shoulder, but then regretted it, making it sound like the coffee was the real problem. But if not that then what? The scotch? At this late date?

"You said he was naked," reminded Rudd.

Carey stared at the man and wondered if his own talents weren't being squandered here. "Green," he said matter-of-factly, a detail. "He was tagged Green. They spray-painted it across his chest the way they do."

Rudd grunted and nodded. He'd be goddamned if he was going to let this twirp get the better of him just because he wasn't up to the minute on the latest pre-teen gang member rules of etiquette. "Poor guy," he said, thinking, I wonder if he was black. Would the paint show up? Green. Son of a bitch. Maybe we should have paid closer attention to the TV. He suddenly felt a need for information, Stay Tuned burning at his back. "What else has been going on out there?"

Hooked like a fish, thought Carey, and Where's my fucking coffee. He looked around for Jill, but saw Tony's instead and remembered for the umpteenth time exactly where he was. And Jesus, talking to a murderer. If I tell him what's going on out there will he let me see his gun? Jesus. Just ask Jill later.

Some hours after the predictably irresolute conclusion of his conversation with Carey, Rudd sat at the bar with Fenton. The television was off now, the men, including Rudd, finally drunk enough to not care much when he shut it down. In fact he had not gotten the chastising reaction that he'd been almost counting on, and was disappointed enough to give the remote a sloppy underhanded toss behind the bar, where it clattered and cracked to the floor. "Show's over," he'd said, but again no reaction. Now he was feeling desperate and close to Fenton, and trying hard to gauge the curve of their relationship. He asked himself: Why would I rather be with Fenton than anybody else here? He asked himself: Would I? He asked himself: Would I give my life for his? He asked himself: Would I give my life for Jill's? Dunno, Yes, Dunno, Think so. There was either an incongruity to be puzzled out in there or another drink. B.

"So," began Fenton, "were you able to bring him around? He gonna go outside and kick some ass tonight?" He smiled broadly, stroking their alliance and smelling of scotch.

For a moment Rudd thought he detected a false note—not

irony exactly, more like acting—but then he realized that his friend was merely drunk, drunk as he was probably. Well good; he'd always felt their relationship could use a little lubrication. "Fucking little geek," he sneered. He reached for the bottle of J&B and splashed some into both their glasses. Outside a gunfight began, making him realize how relatively quiet it had been this day. "Now he's safe and warm with us to protect him so he's getting brave. Getting to be an asshole, in fact. You should hear him; guy sounds like he's running for office on the Bleeding Heart ticket. But you remember how he came in here—hell, I don't have to tell you, you're the one who found him. He was pissing himself to get away from his constituency." Funny: again with the false note, only this time from himself. Yet this *was* him. Was Rudd.

To Fenton the gunfire outside sounded good, like a call to action. "We should go out there," he said, nodding to the shuttered and sealed front door. "I think of how it's been since things started, all the time we've spent in here, and I gotta tell you: the best so far was that run. I was scared to death, absolutely, but it was a thrill. I know for you too, right?"

"Sure."

Simply put, it was. Then came the thing with Jill. Rudd felt a stirring there, not so much better or more exciting than the shoot-out in the street as it was . . . well, deeper, or more permanent. No, it was more provocative. The thing in the street was paper thin. Okay, say there's a moral question for a guy like this Carey, a guy sitting and watching, but being in it was far different, and far more enlightening. Out there as he was squeezing off rounds and watching bodies fall the moral quandaries peeled away thin and whole like onionskins. Pinch, lift a little corner, and wham: a whole level falls off. A shroud. Those bullets rained like a shower, and Rudd was clean and one with the new world, the world now. Fenton too. He was there.

But Jill was more of a hint at a lesson not yet learned, and Fenton was *not* there, thank Christ. That thing with Osmond and Miles—Fenton had told him when he'd come up from dry-storage asking for Jill, who was in the restroom by then, and wondering out loud who the fuck Carey was and how he got in—was more of a statement than an action. Rudd certainly wasn't Oprah, but he knew enough about women, and about himself, to recognize that Jill hurt. What worried him was his complicity. If she was hurting herself with those two goons, was she also hurting herself with him? He thought a lot about that, Carey's presence only complicating matters though he couldn't say exactly how. Being with her alone downstairs he could've sworn that it was working, working the way it was supposed to work. He was sure that she came to him because she wanted to be there. So maybe he was worse than just not-Oprah; maybe he was Geraldo. But back then, back there, when he was working hard to be with her, he felt like Phil. He really did want to be there with her, so why did he feel like a bad guy? Jesus, at least he'd have stopped if he'd known better, more than could be said for Osmond or Miles. Clearly more.

Carey, watching Rudd and Fenton over Jill's shoulder from across the room, was certain they were discussing him. He could hardly blame them. He'd shredded Rudd and sent him scurrying from their conversation licking his wounds. On the other hand, these guys were so pickled that he doubted if anybody noticed or remembered. He had grave concerns about being here. Now that he had a fuller perspective on the difference between Inside and Outside he wondered: was it all that bad? He could split, make it to the Franklin shelter, probably find some friends. There was work to be done out there, would be plenty more as the weeks passed. So what was he doing in here, a place destined to be fire-bombed at any moment. Sitting here, locked in here with these men, no matter how he felt or who he was, to the outside world he was declaring his loyalties, and the fire-bomb wasn't going to pause and tap him on the shoulder, warn him to slip away.

Jill said to Carey, "I still can't believe you were out there all that time. You're so lucky to be alive. That you made it in here, it's a miracle really."

Fenton said to Rudd, "Sure? Is that the best you can do? We really *should* go back out there. Sounds like you could use the diversion too."

Carey said to Jill, "I really only came in for a break until things cool off some out there. It's not *that* terrible. They have shelters. I might go to one, or maybe just back out to see what's going on, especially now with the television off. Sitting in here, how are we even supposed to know . . . well, know. I mean what was the plan? Stay here forever? Until the liquor runs out?"

Rudd said to Fenton, "You might be right. We could use a little information anyway, especially now that I fucked up the remote and we can't Stay-fucking-Tuned. Do you suppose there's anywhere on this street we could find more scotch? I know the liquor store has probably been licked clean, but let's face it: this stuff isn't gonna last forever."

"Okay, thanks," said Fenton. "How should we do it? What should we do?"

It was thus that Rudd came to fully grasp his position, what he had become and where he stood. Heretofore his authority had existed largely in his perception; it was what he wanted. But now Fenton had asked permission to do something and thanked him for granting that permission. It felt like more than he had bargained for—though of course it was exactly what he had bargained for—and he couldn't help but resent Fenton for folding so easily before such a patently unqualified buffoon as himself. Suddenly the voice inside his head grew loud, painfully so, and Rudd wondered if this was what cabin fever was. Maybe, though he'd never taken it seriously, it being one of those quasi-conditions, anecdotal and bearing the smack of an old wives' tale. Once when younger he'd stepped into the ashes of his great-grandfather's barn, a recent victim of arson. They looked hospitable enough, those ashes, but they burned the hell out of his sockless, sneakered foot, and he screamed to wake the countryside. Great-grandma, calmed by prodigious age and bearing encyclopedic knowledge on how to respond to any likely farm or kitchen emergency, stripped off the smoldering shoe and immediately applied a salve of butter, this being an immutable part of her erudition. Mom made to object—Rudd saw her, knew the look—but decided GG's waning authority here might be worth a foot or two of preservation. From here he could see, she salted that scream with purpose, Mom did, the deferential bitch.

Rudd hated almost everything he thought and said, the screams and voices in his head. What was wrong with Fenton that he couldn't see through such a thin veil of power. This whole world was full of bad guys winning by default; then it passes through reality and becomes history and everybody proceeds from there. The thing that had bugged him for years still festered, threatening always to make him ever more reckless: you get what you ask for. This made no sense, this going outside for a walk. There was no booze out there, and if there were any new information they wouldn't be told to Stay Tuned; now *that* machine wouldn't be shut down long because of some damn riot, not with all those ten-, fifteen-, thirty-, and sixty-second spots flitting through oblivion. Best stay here and wait it out, play the booze by ear—there was still plenty of stock down in dry-storage, not to mention all this liqueur shit up here for display, Miles's Choice for now 'cause he knew it rankled, but still it would stave off the DTs if the time came. Rudd thought about the times that would come, opportunities even, what with so much to sort out, all that unfulfilled TV advertising revenue, for instance. And banks, think of the banks, the data-storage vaults and magnetic media that were worth their weight in gold now. Those tapes full of ones and zeros would define the fortunes of tomorrow. Might be a good time, it occurred to him, to make the jump and buy a controlling interest in Hollydale.

"I'll tell you what," he said, after appearing to consider it for a while (even though he really had). "I think we're getting ahead of ourselves—I know I am. Maybe it isn't the best time to be taking foolish risks." He paused, fixed his face with fairness and took some scotch over a staccato bang beyond the door, like: Hear me? See? "Think about it: it's been like what, seven days since the shit hit the fan? Remember those riots in L.A. a long time ago? That was like a weekend plus a day or two I think. And much smaller. What I'm saying is that we're probably coming up on a major turn of events here. I know it seems to get worse every day, and I know we're all going a little stir-crazy; but I've been thinking about this thing with the TV going out." He paused while Fenton drained his drink and refilled both glasses, Rudd watching him in exaggerated detail and politeness. His dad used to watch him like this, official wine steward at fourteen. Go, boy, fetch! "What's more likely: that a bunch of disorganized petty looters with pop guns overpowered the United States Army and took control of the airwaves—for no good reason, mind you; we haven't exactly seen any subversive, revolutionary broadcasts (Rudd averted his gaze casually so as not to risk a how-would-we-know look)—or that the guys on top are three steps ahead of everyone and shut down the broadcasts as a blanket way to silence all those inflammatory local newscasts we were watching? I mean, what was the message going out there? Hey, it's party central down at Stab-'n'-Grab Electronics! Hurry to avoid missing the best selection!" Fenton began to laugh drunkenly at this, and thus encouraged Rudd went on. "Hurry to avoid missing a shot at Whitey while he still got breath in his body!"

But Fenton sputtered out, and Rudd quickly followed. "Are you going stir-crazy?" Fenton asked with a tone so grave it belied the lightness Rudd had been hoping to keep attached to the term, like make it a nice way of saying cabin fever. Fenton waited, listened. This man wanted an answer.

A great thing about alcohol is that it cuts down on a lot of the transition time between moods. No sooner had Fenton pulled taut his face than Rudd was able to perceive the gravity of the question. Stir-craziness: can it be stopped in our lifetime?

"I'm not sure," said Rudd. "I've spent many hours in this place over the years, and it's never happened before." He pondered, extrapolated those years, searched for what was different, where was the control group. Miles and Osmond? Hardly. "Of course I was drunk then," he added. "And I could leave whenever I wanted."

From across the room Carey could identify the sounds of yet another drunken conversation, though he hardly had to around here. It disgusted him that these men had nothing better to do in the face of history than sit around and drink themselves stupid. This place was really eating at him, making him stir-crazy, was the term. Carey wondered how real that was, that idea of stir-craziness. Certainly being confined to a fixed area would affect the mind. He rummaged for historical examples, but all he could come up with was Proust, and Proust did okay for himself. Men in prison, even that worked better than you'd think. Maybe it's a weakness in me, he thought. Maybe I really don't have what it takes any more than I have a gun. It's a new world, the Year of the Fat Dumb

Well-Armed Republican Drunk. Then it hit him: these guys were all drunk all the time. That's why it didn't faze them to be cooped up in here with no end in sight. Besides, they probably all loved the place and would be here anyway. Why else would they have been caught here to begin with? Of course there was Jill. She was pretty much sober as far as he could tell, except for a little something on her breath two nights ago when he first walked in. Something else though about her, she had something working, something in play. To Carey, having just met her but privy to some fairly involved conversations nonetheless, Jill was like those dark and troubled women who haunted poetry readings and pro-abortion rallies, high-mileage women with too much to say in search of a voice with which to say it. Carey had seen such women hurt themselves and once he even helped one do it, knowing he'd end up hating himself later but falling prey to the exigencies of her addictive craving. That wasn't sex that time but it could've been and the distinctions get pretty fine when a pretty little thing mounts a greased slide to hell. Jill was either getting or looking for her fix—one look told him that—and he wanted no part of it. That left only the spooky busboy, who was, if not strictly sober, then at least not drunk, and so embroiled in his own agenda that he likely wouldn't move from that kitchen even if the riots ended unless moving at that moment was part of his master plan all along. That kid might be crazy, crazy from hurt and racial treachery like the revolutionaries outside were, but he wasn't stir-crazy. Besides, if anyone could walk out of here right now he could. No, Carey decided, I'm a special case. I'm the one who doesn't belong here. I'm the one who'll crack first. And he thought about thinking that and he wondered if perhaps it had already begun, that cracking, first.

Rudd and Fenton spent a quiet moment with their drinks, contemplating what wasn't being reported on the vacuous television screen.

"Even turned off that thing annoys me. I should get that kid in the kitchen to take it back, tell him to squawk if something comes on. Why not? He's gonna sit back there anyway, might as well give him a job. Anything to keep him from sending more smoke-signals." Rudd chuckled, breathy and full of scotch, not a guy to sit next to.

Fenton follow-chuckled and added sarcastically, "We could send *him* out to see what's up. He'd blend right in."

Rudd, who was fully prepared to laugh, didn't like that kid in the kitchen. "It *has* been sort of quiet tonight," he said, predictably preceding a punctuational pop outside.

Carey quit his booth to refill his coffee mug. It felt good to stand up and walk; he hadn't realized how long he'd been sitting. Rudd and Fenton were still blabbering except the former had suddenly become contemplative, which was so fucking typical for that kind of drunk. Carey thought, What the hell go over and have a chat while they're still balancing on their stools. They didn't look like murderers, but they didn't look like people he wanted to be in the same room with either. Coming up on them, he said, "I see you've got the TV off again. How we gonna know what's up." Affecting play, he wanted bad to rankle Rudd.

Who did in fact think, Fuck him and his TV. "We can no longer subject ourselves to the lies of the liberal media," said Rudd. "So we were just now considering our alternatives for information gathering." He sipped his scotch, turned, and spread his face into a big grin. "Your input will be most welcome."

Obnoxious. Murderer. "Good timing then. I came over to tell you that I'm going outside for a walk," Carey said, surprising himself more than the two men, who in their state first took the remark for a weak joke.

Rudd couldn't resist, "A walk? Way I heard it you came inside on a run. That right, Fenton? Or did Carey just stop in to use the rest room?"

Fenton was a guy who tried to be pretty agreeable all around, but more and more he found himself being drawn into declarations, just as he was being drawn into alcohol addiction. These were times of acceleration. "Well he was already in when I got there, but I don't think Jill would've opened that door for a light tap and a request for a cup of sugar."

Rudd looked funny like maybe he didn't get it.

Carey, disgusted at this schoolyard banter, smiled sarcastically to predicate his leave.

Fenton said to him, "You were pretty white, man." Close enough and he was gratified to see Rudd laugh. Well, all's well that ends well.

"Okay, fine," said Carey, not taking much trouble now to hide his disdain. "Thanks for your help. I was scared. I'd seen some bad things and I wanted in. Now I think I might have made a mistake. No reflection on your hospitality, but I think it's time somebody took a look outside. Frankly I don't know how you all can stand it cooped up in here. It's no wonder you're all drunk!" Damn. Too far, he thought. I really do need to get out of here before one of them shoots me. I'm better than this, better than them.

"Jesus, Fenton, he's serious," said Rudd, evidently not at all offended by the drunk remark.

Fenton, who was actually somewhat flattered at being referred to as drunk, waxed philanthropic as he extrapolated Rudd's cue into, "Why don't you rethink this, Carey. C'mon, sit down and have a drink with us and we'll talk it over. In fact we were just talking about this when you walked up. Rudd has an idea." He gestured to the latter as he clumsily slid off his barstool and onto the one behind.

Carey, not at all dismayed at the prospect of backing down from the combat zone, made a show of reluctantly pulling the proffered stool out from the line of fire between the two men and into the apex of a triangle. "Thanks. I'll stick with this," he said, holding up his coffee mug.

Rudd and Fenton leaned into him, never realizing, the two of them, how Carey's pronouncement had galvanized their inchoate plan to send the busboy outside as sort of an un(white)manned probe. For all they knew there could be a calvary of Guardsmen set up shop at the end of the street. But the real point was protecting the supply, and even though they were in no immediate danger of running out of liquor, that time might come. The more they knew about the outside world the better choices they could make in here. Of course the choice was pretty much singular: drink. Nonetheless, knowledge was power.

"What we were thinking," began Rudd, trying to look disdainfully amused at the coffee thing yet feeling that nasty nip of envy he rarely acknowledged to himself and never to anyone else and pausing to drink more because this was one of those rare times, "is that *some*body probably should go out there and take a look at what's going on." He cast around expansively: I've thought this through so don't bother to second guess me. "Now you and I have both been out there–"

Carey managed to roll his eyes without moving them, a flutter and a knit. We're in this thing together, Me and Rudd. He looked to Fenton but the problem there was the guy didn't know how to be a drunk. Carey guessed he was new at it, but what the hell would he know. Maybe he himself would be sloshin' down the suds in a week's time. Good thing he wouldn't be here to find out.

"–so I don't have to tell you what it's like."

"It's scary," said Fenton. "Damn scary."

Rudd nodded profoundly. "He knows. He took out his share." He beamed, the proud father.

Jesus, thought Carey. Sitting around chatting with murderers. He kept forgetting.

I am my father, thought Rudd. That means nothing. This means nothing. "No place for a white man." I Spy to Cosby. All those years and all that money, now does he loot or get looted, that guy?

"No. That would be in here, right?"

Fenton and Rudd looked at each other. A trick question? The temptation was to go ahead and let this bleeding heart do some real bleeding, but now the busboy idea was so fixed and the kid himself, rather the idea of him, his inscrutability, had become such an annoyance, such an insult to their sanctuary— the unappreciative prick—that neither of them, or at least Rudd, was about to let it go. Not now, not drunk or sober. Not drunk. Sort of a duty too, protecting this schmuck. Now *there's* a word his father wouldn't use!

"Here's how it is:" came Rudd; then he checked his nascent anger. He reminded himself of all he'd learned about himself during the days since the riot began. "Unless things have calmed tremendously you can't survive out there for five minutes. Nor can I nor Fenton, and we have guns—"

Carey thought, then decided to say, "Has it occurred to you that that might be the problem?" What the hell, it seemed real coming in, so why not make it real going out. He deserves that much. As real as it can be with a drunk at least.

"—and it's because of those guns that we're having this conversation. Without them this place doesn't exist." But as he said it Rudd knew the only ammo they'd fired was when they went out to get more ammo. That was a detail, not germane to this conversation. Privileged information, and he didn't even have to look at Fenton to detect a confirming nod.

"Fair enough," allowed Carey, who really only had experience against this argument when it was in the more abstract arena of imperialism and dictatorships. But here, with this small thing, as far as he knew he'd be dead without Tony's. And Tony's door wouldn't have swung open without those guns.

Whether that meant there'd have been no one to open it or that those who did open it wouldn't have been armed, he couldn't say, much less defend or prove. Life in America. Fair enough. As long as you're on the right side of the liquor store counter.

"You're here now," Rudd told him. "You're welcome to stay as long as you like. Of course. Till it's over, whatever. If you want to leave I can't stop you, but then you won't be here. What I'm saying is when you're here I'm in charge. If you want to be here, good. But I say who goes and who stays and when the door opens." As long as you're living under my roof you'll abide by my rules. Very original, Dad. "I hope you'll stay. I know we can all get through this alive."

Speech sounded vaguely familiar to Carey, said, "Yeah I see, and I appreciate. . . ." He eyed the bottle of scotch. Not really, he thought. "You had an idea?" Just fuck me now. Just stick your gun barrel up my ass and get it over with.

Rudd said, "Had a chance to meet our faithful busboy yet?"

"Don't feel bad if you haven't. He pretty much keeps to himself," said Fenton, grinning.

So what's the point here? thought Carey. I'm supposed to stick around and be minority liaison? Fuck it. He said, "You need me to be Tony's social worker? The microcosmic equivalent of that convenient layer between you and the Great Unwashed? Will you underpay me if I promise to placate this internal potential rioter with passed-along welfare payments to keep him in the jug wine and giblets?"

Rudd laughed; Fenton too. "Well at least we all know whom we're dealing with," said the former.

"He's got his finger on the pulse," agreed Fenton.

Carey merely smiled back, a tad off balance now that these offhand yet derogatory remarks had been taken so well.

Sensing this, Rudd said, "It don't worry me, brother Carey. I've got nothing against the busboy except maybe that he wants what I've got and he thinks that constitutes earning . . . or at least deserving."

"You don't know that. Has he ever told you that?"

"He tells me by not speaking, by not moving from his chosen hideaway back there, by stealing every loose dollar bill he can get his fingers on."

"Oh I see. You've of course invited him out here to spend the evening with you, drinking at the bar?"

"No. But I didn't invite anybody else either."

"It's not the same and you know it."

"My point exactly."

Carey knew better than to let this shit get to him. "Back to your idea?" he suggested after a pause.

"Everybody's here for a reason, right?"

Carey, getting it: "You need some tables bussed? I'll do it."

Later, as Rudd and Fenton briefed the busboy in the kitchen, Carey sat alone in a booth, appalled at his impotence here, the more so because it was such a familiar feeling yet no less frustrating. And, perhaps in this case, criminal. But he wasn't God, and that kid had to say no if he felt no. Carey couldn't tell him how he felt and he didn't have to tell him how he was permitted to feel. You wanted to. But you knew: it only made things worse. Even if Carey charged out the door they'd just write him off—they'd probably be right—and send the kid anyway. Going with the kid would only make them both targets and eliminate any advantage that really did exist in Rudd's skewed logic. This was it. Like everything else, swallow it whole and move on.

Jill watched him brood and knew by some commiserable instinct that he shouldn't be approached. Her eyes stayed open enough around here to also know what Rudd and Fenton were doing in the kitchen, and frankly she couldn't have cared less.

"More important than that," continued Rudd, momentarily preempting Fenton's (who didn't notice much less mind) portion of the impromptu briefing of the busboy apropos of his reconnaissance mission, "is that you get a sense of what's out there. What I mean is, say things are still bad, no troops or cops—" He took a beat to sip his scotch. It hadn't occurred to him until this moment that this kid was as likely to get shot by the good guys as by the bad guys. But the kid wasn't flinching or even reacting so what the hell, probably always ran that risk, Rudd reflected. Just a dash of that, a glimpse of your nose waving from the surface of your drink, a looking glass to go not so much through as in. "—say we have to stay here for a while. Try to see what's out there in the way of supplies. Of course I don't expect there to be much, but maybe that liquor store down the street is still standing; might be a storage room nobody's found—right up your alley," he quipped to no reaction. "I mean you'd know your way around a place like that. Like a job skill." Rudd wasn't penetrating this kid at all, and he looked to Fenton, smiled and nodded in search of an aping confirmation.

"And Simply Susie," said Fenton to the kid.

Not much help and certainly not what I needed, thought Rudd, to whom Simply Susie sounded silly, back-of-the-head familiar, and promising enough to stave off any annoyance he might have felt at Fenton for not keeping up. "What the hell's Simply Susie?" he said.

"A quiet cafe featuring nouveau Franco-CaliforniaMex cuisine," sneered the busboy.

Everything stopped. Suddenly neither Rudd nor Fenton could remember if they'd ever heard this kid speak before, even one word.

"That's right!" said Fenton, a bit too enthused. "That's what the ad says, and I passed the place when I was driving up, just down the block. 'The crowd's almost as good as the food'!"

"Okay, back off, boy," said Rudd, supremely annoyed at this uncalled-for chumminess.

"Well it was a funny ad is all," said Fenton, hurt.

The busboy, summed to zero, returned to his hot-faced smoldering glare. We're in the kitchen, my room, and I've got tricks.

The busboy gave them a look so clearly meant to display impatience that the men weren't sure if he'd spoken words to that effect; unless it was the echo of his one pronouncement, still resounding throughout the kitchen like a gong or the dink of the chisel in the old Mark IV Productions movie logo that these two white men were simultaneously reminded of hearing and watching and not quite understanding as kid and not-so kid. Fenton turned to Rudd and he to him and both turned to the kid who moved so boldly and so unexpectedly (again, as if to underscore his speech) to put his hand on the door handle that the latter two decided they'd had enough and what's done is done anyway.

"You be careful. Try not to take too long," said Fenton, arriving at what Rudd had to admit may have been the perfect thing to say, the best way out, the line the latter wouldn't have found any time soon.

Busboy had enough and now darkened door to night beyond. Fled.

"Say, what's your name kid?" said Rudd to no one in particular.

Dry Sack Canasta Cream Sherry, Duff Gordon El Cid Sherry, Domecq Vina no. 25 Sweet and Mellow Sherry, the latter bearing dust and a ringlet of ossified, sherrified schmaltz twixt cap and bottle, daring entry in the same musky breath of invitation, a chastity belt, a breachable condom, a mistake forewarned, make no mistake.

"How much of this shit is there?" wondered Fenton hours after the busboy had left and some hours after his safe return.

Amontillado Sherry, Gonzalez Byass Jerez Diamond Jubilee Cream Sherry, Gonzalez Byass Jerez Tio Pepe Very Dry Sherry, Harvey's Bristol Fino Extra Dry Sherry, Duff Gordon Santa Maria Cream Sherry, and Harvey's Rich Golden Shooting Sherry all stood thus abreast, awaiting inspection like the whores they were but nix the disparaging smug-'n'-wry smiles of miles worn. Plush red carpet under slipper, gum on both, not so plush my name's Marina, babe. Have a sip but don't touch.

"It's all up here," Rudd told him. "It's all for show at the bar—blue stuff to make the real stuff look appetizing—no need for backstock because nobody drinks it. Downstairs is all *act*ual booze." He paused, looked at the men by way of on-the-line-manship. "I say we drink it. Fuck it." Then added as if it were a logical support of some kind: "Nothing out there, we know that now. Fuck it (Rudd was already . . .). We drink it and save the good stuff for later. Drink it now, all we want. All of it," in fact he said or thought and looked around, "like a mission or something."

Marie Brizard Blackberry Liqueur, Marie Brizard Mandarine Liqueur, Marie Brizard Menthe Liqueur (green), Marie Brizard Maraschino Liqueur, Marie Brizard Menthe Liqueur (white), Marie Brizard Peach Liqueur, Marie Brizard Coconut Liqueur, Marie Brizard Triple Sec. Now these weren't here before,

opined Osmond

(in so many words).

And there was Gaelano Cappuccino Liqueur. And there wuz Cherry Marnier Liqueur. Wuz a bottol of Trader Vic's Rum and Brandy. Got sum liquore Roiano. Gots us da Diana's Old Berlin Cream Liqueur. Suze Centaine, present also, this bottle mostly gone and try to explain *that*!

Reluctantly confessing, Rudd responded, "Okay. You're right. So I found a box or two of this shit in the kitchen and brought it out. So big fucking deal, changes nothing. Best be done with all of it."

And revealed in the course and natural progression of the evening were too a bottle of Verana Liqueur, one of Carolans Irish Cream, which would be fetching a premium price necessitating a glance at the shot list in more economically stable times and presuming a bartender more inclined to glance than the one currently in the freezer. Trader Vic's Navy Grog and Punch Brand Rum was a bottle, Irish Mist Liqueur another. There was Dos Cortados Sherry, Chartreuse Green and Yellow at one hundred ten and eighty proofs respectively, Jagermeister German Liqueur, which was produced in the village of Jill's great-grandfather's mother's birth though no one here knew that, Sambuca Originale Italian Liqueur, Rumple Minze Peppermint Schnapps Liqueur, Gallwey's Irish Coffee Liqueur, Wild Turkey Liqueur, Glayva Liqueur, Cheri Swiss Chocolate Liqueur, and Mandarine Napoleon Grand Imperial Liqueur.

Much later saw Rudd and Miles in a virtual embrace of camaraderie that would mercifully be erased from both their memories by the next day. Osmond regaled Fenton and Langston with jokes he could not remember and ended up telling in something of a reconstructive manner which began with the punch line. Jill and Carey were present largely as observers, the former sipping slowly from something red and syrupy and the latter leaving same untouched after having accepted it only as the quickest way out of further conversation with bartender/pusher Rudd, now in what tomorrow would be revealed as total blackout along with all the other drinking men present. The busboy sat in his place in the kitchen, listened to the men, and sucked from his jug of wine, chuckling derisively at the predictable morning of liqueur-induced white man's burden that was surely imminent. A modicum of marijuana swirled through his system with the wine. It was what he'd gone out for.

Kamora Mexican Coffee Liqueur stood right alongside Kijafa Denmark Cherry Liqueur, near the Malinowa Raspberry Cordial Austrian Liqueur (seventy-six proof), which was set slightly behind the Barenjager Honey Liqueur (seventy proof) from Germany.

Fenton had what one would commonly refer to as bedspins were it in a context more profuse with teenagers, beer cans, and beds. Rudd sternly advised him to have a sip of water between liqueurs, that this would take care of everything and cleanse the palate to boot so that the heady, mouth-embracing taste and aftertastes of the

Wu Chia Pi Chiew Chinese Liqueur

wouldn't be corrupted by the hearty, sing-songy nip of the

Picon Amer Picon French Liqueur. Osmond concurred, and though Miles took exception (Langston abstained) the plan was enacted and Fenton provided with a generous glass of water. Night drew into a tentative morning.

And yet another shelf in a lower cupboard was revealed to contain Peter Heering Cherry Heering Liqueur, a bottle of Bailoni Rare Old Apricot Cordial, one of Venetian Cream Italian Evening, the gem of the cache, and what was this hard-sell stuff doing hidden behind closed door anyhow? Trinca Cachaca, Carmel Rishon Brandy from Israel, Douro Fathers Brandy, ten years old (and then some, no doubt) from Portugal, Orange Liqueur Aurum, Allborg Jubiloeums Akvavit (whafuck?), Dettling Kirshwasser, Liquore Strega, Grappa Julia, Der Lachs Danziger Goldwaffer.

". . . 'cause there's no more chance of making blue ice than there is of making ice blue."

Royal Irish Coffee Liqueur, Sa'ala Coffee Liqueur Cognac, Misimarja Arctic Berry Liqueur.

"I'm saying if the drink is already blue and you put the ice in."

Cuervo Almondrado Liqueur, Yukon Jack Canadian Liqueur, Licor Liqueur Mirabilis 43 Cuarenta y Tres.

"What I'm saying. You're not listening."

Gold Kirsch Cherry Liqueur, Demi-Tasse Coffee Cream Liqueur, Polmos Blackberry Cordial from Poland, Vieille Cure Liqueur de l'Abbayede, Aldof Fuber Achern Cherry Fruit Cordial, Suomuurain Cloudberry Liqueur, Vieille Cure Liqueur de l'Abbayede Yellow, Romona Rum Liqueur, British Navy Pussers Rum.

Creme de Kirsh Liqueur, Bommerlunder Aquavit, Chateau Tanunda Australian Brandy, Brandy Viejo Vergel Dinner.

Soberno Gonzalez Byass Jerez, Marie Brizard Cacao.

Marie Brizard Dark Cacao.

Marie Brizard Curacao, Cherry, Kummel Danoff, and Cream de Cassis.

Sciarada Italian Liquore.

Lamancha Liquore.

Suntory Cherry Blossom Sakura.

Midori Melon Liqueur, Bols Creme de Bana . . .

Two hours later an explosion at an address very near to Tony's woke Fenton from his deep and troubled sleep. First he thought, There's a noise, where would that be on the street; then he wondered about addresses and if such things still existed beyond numbers painted on buildings, if any had relevance. He felt terrible as he lay there in his or someone's booth and felt the building shake gently to rest. This building was now a god to these men. Fenton knew this, knew that its builder's material manifestation of defense against a crumbling savings and loan years earlier had been insane in that it took the shape of a building that would not crumble. He had been right of course; in those days the building *was* the S&L, far more so than the deposits. Some knew it. Fenton himself suspected it. Now the ratchet had clicked quite appropriately and the building was God. It stood between these men of erstwhile wealth and their salvation. Judgment day was beyond these walls, and it wouldn't wait forever.

It took Fenton twenty solid minutes of watching light seeping through a few cracks and holes in the ceiling before he realized it was merely the light of day and not an epiphany from heaven or hell, an angel perhaps to fetch him alone, of all of them, or just a bored angel gone fishin' and looking for the willing nibble of a random soul. Just day.

That's all. Rudd was in charge of this building. Fenton let go of everything and drank something yellow from a half glass on the table above. He lay still and concentrated on keeping it down the way Rudd had advised his neophyte ass. Down it stayed and Fenton was happy to have done well. That's all.

"Good job," said Rudd, slurring whisper, drunk from a nearby booth and surprising Fenton. "I watched you do that. Now I guess I'd better try."

Fenton heard the gurgle and slurp. "Something's different now," he said to his friend.

"Don't be naive," said Rudd, a struggle in his voice, a sureness. "What could be different?"

Day10

The first sign came to Osmond though he failed to recognize it. The television was off anyway, the men having grown weary and impatient and rationalizingly distrustful of the liberal media's test patterns, so that which might have given the day's real news by virtue of its silence was expected to be silent anyway. It wasn't until Langston stepped up to the plate and dipped his hand into the ice machine's cavernous plenum of promise, to the same depth in fact that Osmond's hand had been only moments before, that the first sign was not only revealed but acknowledged. The ice was lower than it ought to be, the blind man noticed without the handicap of compensatory eyesight; wetter too.

Fenton, absorbed in drink and across the room, said (and dig: the light will fade, see, and this dude don't know it), "I miss my books."

"This guy wrote a book that you read it once and it disappears." Rudd said this. This. And he burped. "Maybe no more books. For a while."

Rudd was as shitfaced as he'd ever seen him, Fenton. Said (somewhat shitfaced himself), "I have these books. I read. I was thirty. Twenty-nine. I'd read enough, say . . . say plenty of books, like a few hundred. A few thousand?" He drank more, his eyes swayed without analogy. "Lots of books. I said to people that I'd really read a lot of books. Then I thought, I've read so many books that I've forgotten some of them."

All this time the power's off. For good. All this time Rudd is drunk.

"So if I read so many," continued Fenton, "so many that I'm forgetting them, then why not stop and just reread the books I've already read? I mean, we're stuck with that anyway, right? A little window of creation. We try to fool it with quantity, but the truth is that you can't fool time, and the only way to second guess it is with quality. Those are the books I miss, the ones I've already read. Those are my books. I need to read them again and again." He saw something, something that was too subtle for a drunk man to recognize, yet he saw it nonetheless because it was something that an intelligent man would never miss, like a dimness in the hall when the ladies' room door swung open, or a failure to hum from some fucking freon grid. Don't pay attention. You don't have to. Just take the universe in, blow it out. Look.

"Guy thinks he can make big money with collectors," said Rudd.

"Ephemeral," said Fenton.

Rudd burped again.

Fenton knew the power was out, and for all his mighty thoughts of culture he also knew it all came down to the power, the electricity in that socket.

Life is homosexual rape. I am drunk,
he thought.

"So what's the difference?"—Fenton now—"He makes a book that can't be read again, or I read a book that I don't remember?"

"You're drunk," told Rudd to his friend.

There's a difference, thought Fenton. Maybe the power's out too, he thought.

I'm drunk, thought Rudd. My mind. I should have read more books. He's right. I'm bright. "There's a value in the ephemeral."

"There has to be," said Fenton.

"Everything is," said Rudd.

"Ephemeral," said Fenton.

There was a pause and Rudd felt the power out. Fenton. Guns.

"It's a short time."

RUDD WAKEs Up aNd hshkeas. S khkesa. S. H. A. E. K. S. Enough. Everything, a short time. I sleep, I slept. I sleept (giggle). My god, I need a (G) drink.

It's light enough and maybe he does need a drink. Well of course he needs a drink: he's in a bar. It's a bar. It *is* a bar. Think about all that liquor, there for the taking. A finite amount, perhaps, but there aren't that many men in here. And one of them's a woman, and she doesn't drink so she doesn't count (insofar as liquor distribution is concerned). And one of them's a guy who doesn't drink and doesn't count anyway. Carey, just let him try to take a share.

Rudd, now standing at the service area of the bar, what Jill or the stiff in the freezer, as service staff would call the well, just picked up a fucking bottle of whatever scotch was there and took a long guy-drinkin'-whiskey-in-a-western-movie-bar swill right from the bottle 'cause it was take-what-you-want time—all you want—and there'd be plenty time for crafting selection later. Plenty of ways for a drunk in a bar to define his personality.

Plenty of everything, thought Rudd, getting drunk enough now to think clearly, and if it weren't for Reagan then this place might never have existed. When you think about it. In a twisted sort of way. Or Hollydale. But more scotch, now J&B since our head is clearer, made that thought vanish quicker than a fart in a breeze.

RUDD seated himself at the head of this fine slate bar and felt alone and empowered in the room. The trick is winners and losers; those fucking kids outside can't change that no matter how many guns they've got. It works best this way, a few men at the levers, those who can distinguish between good and bad scotch, cars, automobiles, so on. Hollydale had a limit on how many tee-offs they'd allow so that members were never crowded, and even in that there was a hierarchy, Rudd knowing for instance that he could be worked in ahead of lesser members who had maybe been waiting longer. This way the strong links were placed in the chain by a natural selection of sorts. They would click around that course—Pacemakers, or Pacesetters, is better—click around that course gently (and sometimes not so gently) nudging ahead or pulling along the lesser men, men who would likely in time step up to become the Pacesetters themselves by virtue of their very presence at and membership in Hollydale. A good world, a world that worked then and will work again.

And was working now, for chrissakes, it occurred to Rudd as the J&B flowed like water then some fine twenty-year-old Glensomethingorother into wine. Not his favorite stuff but hey: twenty years old, and who the hell in here is more likely to appreciate it than me. I, make that. Was working now, glitches aside, some green motherfucker stuck in the rough and taking six strokes out. Nudge him along, Pacesetter, shoot a ball his way or see that he waits a few hours for his next tee. There's always a way. Up is still up, even a guy like Rudd couldn't change that, not if he wanted to. Question is . . . but his thought trailed off.

"Power's out," announced Fenton, matter-of-fact son-of-a-bitch, brusquely, from elsewhere in the bar, a place where Rudd was not.

He flicked the switch again, Fenton did, the third one of his confirmatory circuit; across the room, this, and most certainly on a different breaker than dud number two in the kitchen. Wonder if Jill will have enough light in her bathroom, he thought for no reason and admittedly somewhat out of priority. "Power's out," he said again, but softer like to himself. He stood there alone in the corner, a pricey ivory dimmer switch futiley awaiting the tickle of his pinkie.

Waiting, too, was Fenton, and didn't care at all about the power. All things were summing to minor details for him, like he was standing too close to television or French Impressionism. Pointillism. Focus on the end though; he saw it coming, and it was really the only thing to grab for at this point. Best be a part of it. Best keep drinking, learn to catch up. A crash course, going well if you stayed with it and didn't stand back. Fenton strode to the bar for drinks and discussion of power, its outage.

Miles turned curled in his booth and awakened spared the clutch of hangover, quite incredibly, yet cast into the morning's bad news just a second too late to hope Fenton's pronouncement had sprung from a dream. He wanted to panic but had grown accustomed to leaving that role to Osmond's Costello and then playing things a bit cooler. Plus, no lights led to immediate drinking. Somewhat gratuitous perhaps at this point, like creating a flow chart after the program has been coded. Senior year of high school, BASIC, programming in the math lab, Miles remembered, and the only way for him to get the whole flow chart thing was to write the actual program ("Hello, World!") then use it to draw the stupid triangle pictures and arrows. What a waste of time, but the only way he could do it. *Hello, World!* a BASIC statement.

So in the face of the power outage, Miles proceeded directly to scotch. Osmond watched him from Osmond's booth where Osmond had only now opened his eyes and was pretty sure something was up but, having missed the news as spoken, had no idea what it was.

"Miles," said Osmond with some new uncertainty rearing a nose over the old uncertainty.

"Power's out," said Miles, weary enough to not give a shit about parroting Fenton and weary enough of Osmond to not give a shit period.

Scary stuff, and what's more: Osmond knew he was right about Miles, the backing away. Sense it that quick, one thing he was good at. Power's out.

Osmond wanted out of this knowledge, all of it, just as Miles wanted out of Osmond at the moment. He, Osmond, good at the game or at least not without practice in the tenuous affairs of men-friends and surrogate big brothers, tacked eyes down to the bar, tried hard not to quiver frightfully as he took his liquor. A medicinal excuse, always. For him the best. The fat of his belly and his revolvers and the booze, all warming, cooling each other. Warming, for now.

Disgusted, Carey was beyond the point at which reasonable men hold their tongues. Up for hours, watching them all salivate in their sleep, hangovers percolating. Yet all that careful observation and winning the I Found the Power's Out award still goes to a drunk. He wanted so much to. . . . As much as Carey wanted to embrace the apocalypse this little stuff kept getting in the way. So much happening with even more about to happen, a world in flames, and all he could think about was how unfair it was for bachelor number 3 to have made this discovery before he did. So dearly did he deserve to fuck that waitress Jill, and all he could think about was the obfuscation that went with such an act. Find a light switch and you're a hero; fuck a girl and you're a creep. Go figure. Bang bang.

Rang another shot from outside brought a smile to Jill's face—her new habit, did it for some time, she guessed, before realizing it in the mirror one morning, smiling involuntarily (and only lightly) every time the sounds of violence crept in from the outside. Tick tick. Bodies like a countdown, must be outpacing births at this point. Sort of nice in a way, if you think about all that new birthing opportunity being made.

Extra room, she always thought even though everyone told her it was silly, the room problem. Now her bathroom was dark, had been for the longest time. But if she stood still long enough in here she could begin to see a shadow of a reflection (now *that's* silly) in her mirror. Power's out, she'd heard Fenton announce. Yesss, well, it's about time one of them found out. Likely she would have told them eventually, say if some catastrophe had arisen (no, *that's* silly!), but best let them discover this kind of thing by themselves. Sure, she could have told them hours ago. But kill the messenger and all that—if Jill had popped forth with this news they would never have forgiven her for it. Like getting pregnant and taking up the room, in a way it really is all her fault, the bad stuff. Makes sense, and not so bad in the mirror now. Okay: the lighter it gets, the more you can see.

Langston, getting wiser by the second and well convinced by the wetness of the ice hours ago, could nonetheless feel a pang of distress to hear his private power's-out hypothesis confirmed so directly and finally. It would have been better to be wrong about this, but then it would be better not to be blind, too. He wondered if the fires still burned outside after all these days, if the power was really out. Lights out. Lights out, a phrase he may have lived or merely gleaned from fiction, prison movies, tight discipline, boarding schools, military schools, or just his dad. His dad was the type to say lights out, yet Langston can't remember him ever actually saying it. That phrase, almost like life, so tightly woven into his memory it felt, yet he had no recollection of ever hearing it spoken by any live person. A play maybe, still it wouldn't matter. Just like TV, also out. Ironic, this lights-out thing, an augury of sorts, if it had ever been uttered, that is. Well it *must* have been uttered, so it would count, dark man.

Busboy shoulders up to the bar with a thirty-five percent attitude, slips onto the stool to the right of Rudd, who is, to put it mildly, somewhat surprised, is, to put it tipsily, somewhat drunk, to put it surprisingly, somewhat pleased, drunkenly, mildly surprised, ready for a go-around, an unpredictable inventory. Do I talk first or let him? Supposed to know. Something about the advantage. Seize the Day or Tip Your Hand. Impossible contradictions, fit every situation, like astrology or the Bible, cover your ass well with all these republican aphorisms, he had to admit. Useless when the power's out.

"Buy you a drink?" he said smilingly.

For a moment there was a blip, a dysfunction in his drunk. Fact is he felt a loss of control, so normally, familiarly imposed. Something might be lost, panic, bottles, a search for the appropriate republican aphorism. Once saw that mayor in California on CNN, years ago during a brush fire, of all things, places, in Malibu. Guy stands in front of the mansion skeletons and speeches, it's time to pray. Guy was a drunk too, if Rudd had it right. A businessman, made money, enough to get elected. An answer. An aphorism, time to pray, stretched. Well thanks for the good word, Mayor, but I'll still be sleeping in cousin Reginald's guest suite tonight, the bore.

"When you go crazy?" he seemed to want to know, the busboy.

He's already drunk, Rudd could tell right off, not so much because he knew this kid—he didn't know him at all of course–but because he was intrinsically alert to any state of intoxication. It would have been an issue, this kid availing himself of community intoxicants, be they wine or window wash, especially at this late date, but for the remarkable fact of his communication. Rudd thought, let it slide, and sliding himself, said, "But I guess you know where it is," meaning the intoxicants, the more traditional ones.

The busboy responded with a quizzical snarl, like Where what is? meaning the crazy. He looked from Rudd to the bar, the bottles, the tequila, maybe, well. Rudd reached, had to stand but finally grabbed for it, got back with a glass and splashed some in. The kid glanced at it and waited . . . for what? Rudd to drink it?

Busboy left it untouched, left altogether, Rudd alone at the bar. Fuck him, thought Rudd, downing the tequila. Yecch! That'll teach me.

People shuffled and trundled about the room, gravitating toward then often away from the bar but preponderantly toward, looking like a time-lapse security video played out on the television monitor so conspicuously absent from their mid-to-late morning, gone the way of the pleasantries and puffy-face, disheveled-hair smiles and greetings that would accompany such a group were they in a more benign setting. Say a college reunion weekend. A convention. Christmas at home.

Rudd, already at the bar, caught the movement of the tequila bottle in his peripheral vision, but when he looked right at it it was still. Then his glass moved–not much, maybe just a millimeter or so–but again: when he looked right at it, nothing. Onward into the still of his moment the bottles just beyond his direct stare began to tease him, jiggle and dance, move out and back. For a while they did it one at a time but it soon degenerated into a group effort, and Rudd was reminded of apes touching the monolith in *2001*. They played with him in a friendly enough way and he was drunk enough to not feel the panic that such events might warrant. He found he could control them, look away from a row of bottles deliberately as sort of a tease, getting them to do their thing and look back real quick, catching them. Fooling them. It got to be kinda fun and after all . . . why not? It got to be so that when the moment waxed not so still and he could feel the motion and We're-Here-edness of the others his first impulse was intrusion. They want to fuck with my head, he thought, and realized too late to test the limits of his new game that the bottles had, with military precision, stood down.

"Langston said he saw the bottles moving," a voice from behind, feminine, Jill's.

"What!" with a start and turning his neck so fast that it moved within his collar slicker than a ball-bearing primed with sweat and grime and ten days' self-righteousness Rudd yapped.

"What what?"

"What about Langston? I mean he's fucking blind! How could he see anything, much less the bott—" He turned quickly back around. Again that grease. Bathe. Drink more. Do Something!

"No shit, Sherlock," she said, and it amused her to feel so young, to say something you'd say in high school. She giggled.

That giggle burned the back of his neck. How much had he said? Did he tell her he'd seen bottles dancing around the bar like he was some fucking old wet-brained DTer chained to an iron bed in a 1940s evils-of-alcohol movie? Was that why she was laughing at him?

"I mean he's fucking *blind*!" came an echoing roar from down the bar, an outraged Langston, either at the remark or the truth of it, would evidently have a few things to say about what he'd heard.

"Langston," said Rudd, for lack of a better idea.

For the same reason that Osmond rose from his stool and lumbered over to the suddenly diminutive-appearing Miles, took the latter in his big bear arms and the man embraced never looked less likely to speak.

Thus the collision of smart-ass and fat-ass, thought Carey, and no matter who knows what first, I'm pretty much the god of this place. I mean really. And seriously. Thus he spake in a whisper of utterance, "I, God," and he pondered the little universe of colliding particles before him. Of all present the room was best—by far—understood by him. Him. That would be the definition.

Carey looked up to find Fenton staring right at him.

Not much of a man, that guy, thought Fenton, just like me. He was pretty sure that his dad wouldn't give a guy like Carey the time of day. Even Rudd couldn't stand the guy. Fenton felt in a way cast by his dad and painted by Rudd, but he felt nothing for the shifty-eyed little creep with whose eyes his were locked. Now said creep looked down, breaking the lock, and they both knew that meant Fenton won; so that was one at least.

Fenton tossed back his share of the waning supply of J&B, not sure if he needed to want it or wanted to need it. A right of passage, like newlyweds smearing wedding cake on each other's faces, it made him want to back away, to run and wash it off instead of laughing stupidly at himself along with the rest of the badly dressed room. But you gotta go with the bride and Rudd had fairly ordered for him how many days ago: from now on we'll *both* be drinking like men, son; no more of this soda pop.

Pop pop pop pop. More guns, real or merely in his head, he couldn't tell anymore. Fenton licked the sweat from his upper lip and hoped no one had noticed him tremble, drank more scotch and heard more pops. All the time now, they scared him. He felt for his Glock, caressed it like a penis (a scared kid, thunder maybe, he remembered, at some point inevitably he'd discover his hand on his dick, sometimes squeezing–*pop*–sometimes so hard that it hurt and that would be what tipped him off). How had he come so far? Arrived at this point in time from some . . . well, if not happier then at least safer point in time. The whole thing was a wrong turn, a mistake he'd made sometime long ago. Probably something small, tiny, infinitesimal, that set off the chain of events that brought him here and deprived him of his real life. Now he found himself growing numb–no, more like suddenly numb. Just yesterday he stepped away from the bar and into a pocket of still, stale air that happened to be whatever temperature is exactly neutral to one's body; that is this place in the room was of such a temperature so as to feel neither hot nor cold, not the slightest bit. It felt like nothing, at once alluring and repellent, that sensation. Lack of sensation. *Pop pop pop.* Novocain in the mouth—*pop*—residually lingering as one limps from a dentist visit—*pop pop*—is what he was reminded of by that air pocket. Sip a cold soda, unsettling as hell, good to have a brain at a moment like that to tell you everything's okay; otherwise you're a cat with tape on its paw. And still, with the soda, you gotta keep it on the feeling side of your mouth. But like with a soda Fenton couldn't resist stepping into that pocket of air yesterday. Not so much unsettling, it turned out, but it did break his heart. Pop.

Jill, still laughing, albeit more inwardly, standing near Rudd, noticed the momentary eye contact between Fenton and Carey. Convinced it had something to do with her, she knew it was crucial now that she appear very much at ease with the situation. Play it cool and ride the laugh—whatever it was about—was her strategy. She tried desperately to remember whom in this room she had fucked. But answers such as those always hurt too much on arrival, like a baby would, she supposed, so she'd long ago learned to pretend that much of her life hadn't happened. A defense mechanism of sorts, it left her with only causeless effects, monsters' shadows against the wall with nothing there to cast them.

Outside before the apocalypse, which is what she'd secretly decided was occurring, Jill had taken to spending most of her time in her apartment. Some new place, she'd try now and then going out with a friend, would be a ticking clock for her, counting down the weeks, days, or hours until she did something to herself in that place, usually with the assistance of some willing and not-so-caring accomplice. Then would begin the slow burn, hotter and deeper each time she went back to that place, until the inevitable time came when it was simply too painful to return. Thus again and again she decreased the size of her universe, eliminated options. And as they waned, those options, and she was left with fewer and fewer painless locations she began to notice that even these latter had taken on a patina of the burn, a fine ash, due to their very exclusion. The ephemeral nature of any place free of past terrified her. She felt as though she were standing on a sinking island, and it was then that the fabric of her master plan for herself was revealed. Jill knew that she could never kill herself; the next best thing was to systematically render the world untenable. It was time to cut deeper, and she began inviting men home with her and soon found herself sleeping on her own sofa.

Ironically it was because she'd taken to picking up every available shift that she—for better or worse—was holed up at Tony's now. She wasn't scheduled to work at all the day the apocalypse started, but she'd planned on it just the same and sure enough one of the waiters asked her to cover his shift at the last minute. He'd decided to go camping after all. Jill wondered where he was at this minute, if he and his friends had made it out and if so to what? A safe place? There would be trees and maybe a forest, where that waiter was, but no food and other problems that seemed now about as relevant as the problems of the people in the third world. For Jill, at that point, the day the apocalypse started, Tony's was a safe place. She'd taken care not to spoil it—work made it relatively easy—and she'd come to (at that point) regard it as a haven of sorts. Ironically.

But the apocalypse changed all that and made her ruin this, her last refuge. No longer could she get wrapped up in the petty complaints of some jerk or jerkess fresh out of assertiveness training with nothing better to do with their time than contemplate the subtle variations of shades of pink in the center of their steak or the degree to which a glass should be polished or the oxidation of coffee, the likelihood that all decaf comes in green-topped carafes, that all service personnel are driven by the need to deceive. These things used to cloud her mind and shield her from actual problems and real pain. It was good, her being here, so as long as her luck held she strove to keep it small and pure, to not spend any time outside of Tony's with the people she knew inside of Tony's, to resist the occasional invitation to a dark corner of the kitchen from the beckoning finger of the occasional heterosexual waiter. It all worked so well. Then the apocalypse made it impossible for her to go on like that. Even before it was too late she knew it was too late. The moment things started to fall apart outside she searched herself for an appropriate response inside, and when she couldn't find one she searched for any response. That she found. It didn't take long to realize that every relationship in this room was about to change drastically and there was no escape. She wasn't about to wait around for things to sweep her along when she had the means to control it all right from the start. She wasn't about to wait around for the silence. These guys would take any coffee at any temperature from any carafe and be glad to get it. These guys would be too wrapped up in their developing agendas to think twice about coffee or who brought it to them.

But that was good. But that was bad. She didn't know. She never had. Jill thought it best now to move gently away from Rudd and to keep laughing but not talk to anybody as she made her way to her bathroom because it would be best now to get a look in the mirror and not talk to Rudd or the other men was what would be best now though it seemed that he was annoyed and seeking an explanation. "He's blind," she probably said or at least thought and wondered how long before even her bathroom was a place she couldn't go. She could take him there now. Or somebody else, somebody who'd not had her yet. If only she could remember who was left. Ask them, they would know, but then they might not go. If it came to that. Or giving head in the bathroom. Her bathroom. Get a grip, give her a handle on the day. They'd always do that. They wouldn't care at all. She could be a legend. She could be a joke to them. Become something. Then go out for a walk and become something else.

As Jill walked by him, giggling and on her way to the ladies' room, Rudd almost said, I know he's blind. But it seemed petty and she was upset about something despite her laughter and it might be best to leave her alone for now. Rudd wanted badly to share with someone the phenomenon of the dancing bottles, and Jill would be the one to share it with. Her laughter notwithstanding, he was pretty sure that he hadn't mentioned it to her—but then he was pretty sure he'd seen bottles dancing around on the bar. Intellectually he knew it wasn't a likely occurrence and that it would be a good time to arrest his senses and consider how much of this was about alcohol and how much about the demands and pressures of the situation. Jill, being a woman, would be the choice to confide in. Less of a chance of open ridicule or even concealed contempt, questions and doubts about his leadership, his manhood, and his right to carry a gun. That laughter was a weapon, intellectual and notwithstanding.

"I am a quiet man, forthright and true," thought Rudd, and then he realized from the sound of his own voice that he had not merely thought this but had spoken it aloud. He decided to heed the laughter and the bottles and not mention it to Jill for what might in fact be the second time.

He downed his drink (or maybe poured a new one and downed that), and as the myopia of the glass's bottom fell away to reveal the room Rudd realized that he must speak to someone about the dancing bottles and that someone would be Carey.

Milling about a tight little circle at the other end of the bar, end for worker bees as opposed to drinker bees, was Carey, the object of Rudd's intentions, basking in his newly found perspective and wondering hard how not to spoil it, wondering hard if it was time for him to embrace the *apocalypse* (a term Jill had let slip during one of their talks); in his new position it might be the prudent choice. Now Rudd's getting up like it were some sort of tag team match in professional wrestling, pushing the envelope of eye contact, taking steps. Carey prepared for a biblical stand in the service well, waited. A waiter. A worker bee. An employee of man, God would be if he existed more as god. A fine line, a fine figure.

I'm cutting a fine figure, he thought, I'm cutting out of school. A school of fish, something about Jesus and fish. Should have read more Bible to prepare for a role in the Third Testament, closest thing to notes. Maybe Rudd will want to be a scribe, write it on a notebook computer. Future millennia will unearth diskettes instead of scrolls: the Book of Marx, the Book of Reagan.

Carey turned upon the damp rubber mat beneath his feet; it oozed unctuously along, cooperatively employing years of Stubborn Greasy Buildup recently reactivated by a late-night pee courtesy of Osmond and a nearby pipe bomb, which the others had slept through. Carey knew all such mats to give a little slip (because this is what one would expect) and thus dismissed it along with the faint scent of urine that had been tickling his nostril as the Way Things Are in Here, pronounced it so with a feckless wave of his arm gone south, returning from an ear scratch.

Rudd approached Carey wondering if he wasn't looking a tad bloated or if Rudd had merely never paid much attention or been this close; he couldn't remember at all and could guess even less.

"So," began Rudd amiably enough, "you caught any of this cabin fever yet?"

"What's that mean," challenged Carey. "Because I had a couple of drinks? I'm not you, Rudd. I'm not a drunk. Why does everybody assume that everyone else must be either drunk or gay or codependent or racist or whatever the hell your personal hang-ups are. All of the above?" He cocked his head and thrust forward his chin, affected an aloof expression he'd once seen and liked in a photograph of himself taken without his knowledge at a friend's house (though he knew photographs were being taken that evening). "I walk above it all, Rudd. I walk alone."

Something that sounded like a mortar exploded outside the door, rocking the building and providing everyone with the loudest noise in the last few days.

Rudd, alarmed at Carey's vituperation, said, "What the fuck."

To which Carey misplacing the antecedent, responded, "It's nothing. It's another fucking gun. What else is new." and, realizing (with some gratification) that he himself wasn't the least bit shaken by the blast, added, "Getting jumpy?"

"I . . . I don't know," said Rudd. He looked at his drink.

Disgusted, Carey told him, "You're a drunk."

Rudd looked from his drink to face the accusation, irrelevant, as hollow as the ever-expanding vacuum of experience beyond the walls of Tony's. The curve of silence out there, he knew, would weather the spikes of an occasional glass-shattering concussion.

Carey saw the man before him as a prophecy about to be fulfilled. All of them, in fact, would perish here, and it was his duty as the observer to not be a part of that, to take his leave so that the events of this place might achieve their actuality, their place in history such as it is or will be. He would be the orchard keeper to their falling apple tree; he would be the one who heard it fall, whose presence demanded that it make a noise. That's why, Carey now understood, it was his lot to leave. The watch is wound, the bang declared big. Leave them here so that they might wind down in peace. Entropy Rules. Decay Kicks Ass. Carey felt—no, *was*—utterly possessed by his thoughts.

Rudd said to Carey, "You don't walk on water, son."

A superficial smoothness settled about Carey as if his face had been heated almost to melting, softening the wrinkles, softening the questions. "You are here," he said. "I'm not." And he spun away from the orbit, into perhaps the kitchen.

You are here, thought Rudd. You Are Here. Like a mall directory kiosk, or the parody of one on a tee shirt he once saw of the Milky Way with an arrow indicating where our solar system is: You Are Here. But the fabric of one is not cut from the cloth of the other, and there is an implied omniscience in the mall that does not exist on the tee shirt, making the former, the mall directory, something of a cheat. Of course you are there. You must be there to be reading the sign. So it works because the sign is in a fixed location, and so, because you are reading it, are you. No fountain of information there, no revelation for the weary. In fact the parody on the tee shirt is really the smallest scale possible for that sign to have any meaning, given that it requires an all-inclusive map from a far away perspective and that you could conceivably be elsewhere in the solar system, here at the dawn of the new millennium. Yeah, that's about as much detail as you can usefully get out of that map, the tee shirt version. One human to another. One human, no matter where he possibly is, to any other human anywhere. That's it, that's the most information that can be provided, your position in the galaxy, You Are Here. Anything else requires an assumption, a guess, or a lie.

Carey, in the kitchen indeed, let his hand drift over the unseemly surfaces of the pots, pans, and various cooking apparatus, the insult of these things. This kitchen looked like a kitchen looks; not like a kitchen looks in the womb of Armageddon. But kitchens are kitchens, and he supposed they have little reason to look any other way and less reason to exist without someone around to require them. He'd worked in a kitchen once, one night, as a dishwasher. One night because he was the busboy and covering the regular dishwasher's shift in a pinch and swore never again, it was. A seafood restaurant, where he worked, and all that night into the morning hours he scrubbed fish pans, pie tins really, used to cook each fish order before being tossed over to him. Hell's acre, those pans, the flesh of his young hands traded for a scratched semi-gloss on a twenty-cent aluminum disk. And the fucks in the overpriced dining room not even knowing of his sacrifice, or worse: assuming it, taking it for granted.

Carey let fall his hand, absently knocking a ladle and tin cup, clanged into the sink. He traversed the greasy floor and breathed odors of things gone bad, thought of water and called it a supper. The locks on the back door required some fiddling but eventually yielded to his exit. Peace in the parking lot backside, light framing him on its way from a streetlamp.

Carey passed away from Tony's. Rudd, catching the last moment of his act, let it be and made his way to relock the door only after sufficient time had been allotted for Carey to not return in a panic. But that lot and light were magnets, Rudd knew, and in or out, really, at this stage of the game was a mostly moot point.

Day15

Fenton had a ridiculous worst-is-over sensation when his eyes opened. Everyone at Tony's had long since been sleeping on a day/night schedule, and Fenton was no exception. Now when he woke he didn't think so much about what time it was but more about whether it was wake time or dream time—not such an easy problem due to the fact that one might encounter the same riddle lurking in a dream; the fact of the question was no answer. Cogito ergo sum. He helped himself to a generous drink though he knew the dwindling alcohol supply had become a matter of great concern among the men. And him too, thus the thirst, the greed. Fleetingly he considered the room downstairs—still an enormous amount of liquor—and just as quickly realized: not nearly enough.

Random firefights outside had increased in frequency. He had no clue why this would be the case. The original battle over perhaps? Renegade factions now warring with each other? Me and the others, these people in Tony's and others like them sequestered around the country or world, now we're the germ, the foreign object, the pocket of resistance facing an inexorable fate. Like always.

Two, three shots, maybe it was, before Fenton realized that some of the gunfire was coming from inside the room, from one of them; *friendly*, it would be called technically.

"Miles! You asshole!" screamed Rudd from down and away, off the bar and in a booth. He gave it a beat of evident consideration before lunging belaboredly (but still impressive for a man in his condition) from the comfort of his drink.

Fenton, not at all surprised over Miles's outburst (or answer), checked out and left Rudd to handle it unobserved, returned to his thoughts which fell on that guy Carey and how very dead he must surely be by now. Fenton saw that his own days couldn't be any more numbered, much as the few remaining bullets in Miles's pocket. Two and a half clips, if memory served. Less now, and those weren't capacious clips. He considered slipping off to the bathroom again and jerking off; but really, the emptiness at the end of that adventure would be more than he could stomach. Firefights now, a better lesser sin.

"Idiot!" slapped Rudd, but not with his pistol hand.

Miles's head snapped to the cuffing.

In the kitchen the busboy's ears lit to the sound of futile discipline; familiar, it brought a smirk. He finished the last of his stash by chewing the roach down to a few shreds of pulp between his teeth and rose from his sore ass feeling arbitrary and weak. Busboy kicked around kitchen like it was some sort of McDonald's Funland mini park and he was the fucking Hamburglar.

Wine down, gone long and now no more shit either, he crackled and spun the cap off a last bottle of cooking sherry, took a long greedy drink from this bottle which at once represented both his autonomy and his limits. Somewhere some days back an uneasy pact had been drawn between him and the others, meaning Rudd, though the latter was only lightly aware of this bargain and the former barely more so. Rudd would never admit that the kitchen wine had been surrendered to the busboy; in fact if he walked in right now he'd need to make a scene and snatch it away (actually just admonish against a repeat incident). But then Rudd wouldn't walk in right now; this much the busboy knew he'd won. But it was strictly limited to *this much*, for *this much* was about to be history, and the real liquor, the whiskey and vodka in the other room was as far out of his reach as the beer in his father's refrigerator would be (if his father or the fridge still existed). Those men out there would shoot him for a drink. A cuffing. He'd have an easier time fucking the girl, a thought that made his head spin against the receding tide of possibilities. The busboy knew that things here were pretty much over.

In his impairment he found an erection between his own legs and boldly, carelessly freed it into the thick air of the kitchen. Holding it, he hobbled over to the freezer door, which punched itself open in response to his hip-smack on the release lever. The busboy stood hard in the not-so-cold musty breath of the silent freezer. Power gone, it had become a giant icebox and by virtue of abundant insulation had managed along quite well until this moment. A matter of time now hastened, busboy breathed unfazed the mildew of incipient honest-to-god rot, the bartender's body, stupid dead white man, defeated, shot, a mere shape in a dark corner. The busboy's erection awakened further to the cool air and the organic, heady odor. He began to slowly stroke himself, and upon this scene stumbled Osmond. White with fear, he trembled huge at his discovery. The busboy sneered and aimed his erection at tremulous Osmond, whose own guns, though strapped securely in place, were a million miles away from his position. Ronald had at last arrived in Funland.

Jill, away from the men by design, sat cleaning her gun, formerly Langston's Beretta, in her booth. She was not aware that Osmond was about to be raped in the kitchen; in fact she didn't know or think much about Osmond at all. He was her brother, in a family-of-man sort of way, and perhaps at times he was her sister, in an unlikely-twist-of-fate sort of way, but the truth is that the two were so very much not destined to have their paths cross that not even a fat two weeks living in the same room could get them to notice each other in any but the most perfunctory way. She had the Beretta field stripped, but when a lone shot outside, more noticeable for its exclusivity than any possible threat it might pose, punctuated the moment it took her far less time than it would have taken Langston on a good day to reassemble the pistol, chamber a round, and spit an answer across the surprised heads of the men and into the quiet side of the front door. Nobody said anything and everybody tried to pretend it hadn't happened though the only one who might reasonably not have heard it was Osmond, whose mind was quite some distance from his own twin revolvers hugging his rib cage and in any case certainly not anywhere registrant enough to pick and place a shot fired to and from someplace as irrelevant as the next room. Osmond, now crippled by terror, was by no one's account a fast thinker.

He, Osmond, and the busboy began moving in a choreography of inevitable descent, swirling for an audience of only themselves to blame, big guns rockin' hard at Osmond's side, banging his ribs. Busboy stilled Osmond's Smiths with a hand on each stock, gave tug as if to pull them away but didn't remove them from their holsters. His eyes said, See what I can do? Now see what I can do, his erection said.

"This gun is mine," he said, the busboy, as he released his grip on the Smiths, not taking them. He'd slurred his words (in his fashion); this told him just how very fucked up he was. Just as he expected. Still, his erection felt as if to burst.

The busboy slapped Osmond with the flat of his right hand. His left followed Osmond's shoulder lower, lower. Osmond felt to gag. There were tears welling in his eyes. He thought of himself, and he took his medicine. It was unlikely that, tomorrow, the busboy would remember any of this. Gunfire sprinkled the night outside; more than usual hitting various outer walls of the building. Osmond quaked, unable to catalog his terror, his anguish. The busboy spasmed, slapped again and pulled away, stumbled backward and tripped against a stainless-steel sink under which he began snoring a vacant sleep. Drunk, dirty, late in the game, and fucked, Osmond gulped. Swallowed. Yeah. Yeah.

Time passed as his assailant snored, Osmond watching, lost, and things in Tony's stilled quiet for a while. Like TV shows, he thought, like being with Miles, like a craps game or the video keno, something happens then nothing happens until something happens again. Waves. Swept, he was, and seated, backed against the worrying nip of a folding chair at his calves. He'd taken the suggestion, seated himself and let the time pass, this nothing time.

Rudd was drunk enough when he stuck his head in the kitchen to not notice or care that anything out of the ordinary had transpired. It was a long-dead proposition in any case, this out-of-the-ordinary stuff, having no real ordinary to be out of, and Rudd never stood too long in front of a painting in the best of times, preferring to walk by with pauses and glances, wait for companions at the end of the corridor while exchanging evasive glances with the security person, and there's a bench for those with time to spare.

"How 'bout you join us for a few minutes in the bar, Osmond. I want to talk about something," he said instead of *What are you doing sitting in the kitchen with the kid?* which would fit what he saw but be inappropriate for what he wanted to know.

Osmond, as if jarred away from a more private concern, left the sanctioning bleeps of the video keno machine and widened his eyes for Rudd. "Okay."

Rudd nodded once back: right. Osmond witnessed his absence and broke his own fear (like a sweat or a fever) of the Thing He Wouldn't Do because now it seemed like anything goes and what the fuck and live and learn and a penny saved and on and on. So he left the kitchen and lumbered down to dry-storage, where Rudd wasn't. Where nobody was because everybody was in the bar waiting for Rudd to talk to them all. And when he was done in dry-storage he would join them.

Despite the foreboding empty spaces on the shelves—due mostly to the men's frenetic consumption of liqueurs and like lesser-grade liquors some days before, got through in a hurry, as if to fully define the parameters of the coming desperation, to let there be no questions, to let there be no mitigation when that time came—dry-storage was a comforting place when Osmond stepped into the dimly lit little room, cool in its detachment (your basic basement vibe, was a thought Jill had left here once). Osmond marveled at all the unguarded liquor, like a store with no clerks and him with no money, which was somehow a tastier fantasy than the reality of clerks and plenty of money to make them give you whatever you wanted. Osmond missed that thought, the one Jill had left lingering on these shelves (though likely he had a tantamount tinge, something cranial), but he did have something new for this party. The bottles awaited, watching, a patient if fatalistic audience. Would he get it? Osmond turned and stole a TV glance over his shoulder, histrionic like a move out of a BBC drama, hollow British videotape going out to almost no one on PBS like a Bible thumper in Times Square. Was someone there? No. Just the bottles, who waited, amused in their fashion. Not someone, stupid. Something, thought Osmond, will happen here, and it will be bad and it will be big. Now it was colder, more like a basement, and he decided to hurry up and do what he came down here to do before this big bad thing happened and he got blamed for it. Then he trotted up the steps. The move was familiar, grownup talk in the distance, a private world.

So the gang's all here, was Jill's thought as Osmond turned into the room from the stairs below, no one knowing where he'd been, what she was thinking, no one caring, all drunk, one way or another.

Rudd began, "Okay . . . ," but then paused as Osmond made his way to the bar for a drink.

Rudd coughed awkwardly, punctuating what little rhythm he'd gained, and the whole scene took on the feel of a keynote address in some Holiday Inn conference room. Hello, my name is Rudd, would have been funny and perhaps elicited a giggle had it been spoken if not for the fact that such a situation was too far away from this new reality, too surreal and, as ridiculed and fatuous as that convention conference room may have been, too longed for. Osmond got his drink all fixed up, near the end of that line, that drink as a point, that line as a segment. He was pretty damn drunk like they all were. Hard to think about Osmond any other way than drunk. Or any of them, any other way than pretty damn drunk. Except Jill. A sort of normalcy at hand, as if one of them suddenly sober would be about as appropriate as a naked guy at a convention. Follow suit. Wear it. The shoe fits. The fit fits. We're drunks. Were drunks. God. Heaven. The Earth. The Past. A line segment, dummy. Were drunks, getitOsmondhiccuppedordid-hehiccough?

Tink tink tink, were it only a spoon on a glass, a rumble to a murmur to . . . patience.

Also sprach Zarathustra. Began Rudd: "Something is rapping on the door of our cozy little world," while breath was held. It was weird, the way he said it, like he really *was* giving a formal speech. Let it go, something told him. So tone dropped, shirt and shoulders let down: "Whaddawe gonna do about all this shooting at the door lately?"

He looked at Jill, who said, "Shoot back."

This was new, not so much for Jill but for the men who peered at her through their alcoholic skulls, the men who had forgotten that every world has parameters, be it a planet or a room, and guns could be used inside as well as out. The isolation of Tony's, all the fire from outside, some directed inwardly, had changed their mindsets since the night—it now felt like years ago—that they boldly sortied forth to retrieve the ammo from their automobiles in enemy territory. That was a great night, and it led to some great drinking. That night was remarkable and tight, like the end of an act in a play; it tied things up and validated so many of the decisions that had been plaguing them like the worrisome tentacles of some bigger and badder insect clicking just beyond the doorjamb. Do I go in? *Swish swish, click click:* this is not a human thing. They drank that night in glee over the command they'd seized, a rule over which they might measure their own situation, ephemeral, like everything else only tighter. Wise men and there was, at that time, a plain of options spread out before them, a vanishing point that could only be approached and never touched. Light, or at least Not Dark.

Yet though again he saw this light, Langston went, "Why?"

"Because we have to make a stand," said Jill.

"Let 'em know we're here," added Rudd.

"They already know we're here," retorted Langston. "And I wish they didn't."

"Hell, there is no *they*," said Fenton. "I'd be very surprised if anybody out there has passed this door twice. There's no organized intelligence plotting against us, no community. That's the whole problem."

"Nonetheless, we might need those bullets later."

Now here was sobering thought, spoken finally by Langston, more frightening for the *later* than for the *need*. The *later* was no good. The *later* made everything seem useless, added an unwelcome fatalism to the drunk, a splash that diluted whatever alcoholic euphoria that was left to be had as surely as would a half can of 7-Up. The *later* was there, a certainty. No telling what form it would take, but it loomed nonetheless. Dry-storage held only so much liquor, and no matter how careful they were—and they weren't all that careful—they would run out. That was one *later*. Tony's was only so well armored; almost bunker-like, but a door is still a door, and there was an endless supply of knockers out there. Another *later*. We run out of water. We run out of food. The power is cut and winter comes. We run out of ammo. Maybe we run out of ammo because we kill each other. We all go insane. We fail to. More, another, another, and another. How about the army finally wins, does something, swoops in, rescues, rushes us all to a hospital for recuperation. Okay, wait for that. How long since anyone actually had that thought. Right, there you go: a not-possible *later*.

Fuck-it-mood Rudd decided to ride the surf. "No. I'm saying how it is: We shoot back. From now on every time that door gets fired upon we answer it. We gotta *do* something. We gotta *be* something, even if it's just a noise. At least we'll for sure be here doing this."

The men fell silent, and so did Jill. For some reason—perhaps it was his blindness—there was a gravitation of glances toward Langston. He twitched in his darkness, and everybody looked away, embarrassed. But Langston twitched a lot; he was a hard man to keep drunk, keep out of withdrawals, so deep was his addiction, so towering his tolerance. Langston would go down before any of them, Rudd knew, and he would go down hard and fast, sweating, trembling, screeching at whatever a blind man thinks he sees or hears while in the throes of delirium tremens. That's what stood at the other side of that room full of liquor down the stairs, behind all the bottles. Langston's demise. Then Miles or Osmond, maybe Rudd himself would be second. They were all far gone, even Fenton appeared to have somehow accelerated his condition; not unreasonable under these extraordinary circumstances. Some of them might die of heart attacks—DTs had something like a twenty-five percent mortality rate, Rudd had once been told in the hospital—some of them might burn through it and get clean, though that was hard to imagine and even harder to hope for.

For the first time in his life Rudd found himself wishing for death, hoping (praying?) that the walls came down before the liquor ran out, that they were stormed, bombed or shot in some truculent surprise attack, some irresistible force, divine intervention. This scenario was not to be their lot, their final act, and Rudd knew that. It would be too easy. Divinity—and surely even the most Divine would struggle at the idea of doling out so kind an ending—was long since a shadow for Rudd. Any god he'd ever had the opportunity to pray to had been wholly, arrogantly abandoned. Part of him regretted his past numerous and emphatic denials, but that was over. Way water-over-the-dam over. No, not Rudd. No Rudd god.

At least they were not alone. Their militia was a paltry one, and that was okay because it still was one, armed and dangerous (to themselves?). Ready to shoot, these men. The Magnificent Seven, these men. That's a Man son, Rudd's dad now. These men knew fear on many levels, shooting and getting shot not among them, but much of the former would be done to protect their liquor, to be sure as much as was necessary. That holy water being the only thing worth defending. The few, the proud, the drunk. We're looking for a Few Good Drunks. And it was with these brave thoughts they sat together drinking scotch. The Scotch Brigade. King J&B need have no fear, his defense was at the ready.

And very drunk they did become. Even Jill joined in with a toast of scotch, not so welcome in the camaraderie. But that was okay because she had a gun and she shot the gun and she shot her Jill gun first. And the men knew that too.

It was Miles who shot the next knocker, or so he thought 'cause this knocker knocked only for Miles. But Miles was a myrmidon and he had his orders. Answer all fire the rule, sobeitbygoddammitillshootthefucker. Miles now. And he returned that imaginary fire as he had before with wild trajectories hitting all surfaces of their altar, improbably missing any of his cohorts. This show was not intended for Langston, who had become dead drunk and passed out some time before (now). This was for the others who were in a condition similar to Langston's just prior to that passing out and therefore too drunk to attempt an admonishing of the extent Rudd had so authoritatively dealt before. But none of the men (or the busboy, who had come out to see what all the commotion was—was enough to wake him from one hell of a drunk as you can get on cooking sherry and fucking a poor fat white fuck) were surprised to see Jill raise the Beretta and fire one shot which neatly pierced Miles's shoulder and brought his inane fire to a halt.

A silence ensued. Miles slumped onto the bar. Jill stood and walked to the ladies' room. Langston did not move. The busboy went back to the kitchen (an erection beginning despite the half-drunk hangover). Miles offered a laugh, a moan, to embellish the situation. Osmond poured more liquor for himself and Fenton, priorities dammit. Rudd, with admirable deliberation, stood and made his way to Miles. In doing so, he did not forget the J&B on the bar and a thought went with him: To sterilize (but really to drink 'cause I'm really gonna need a drink when I see what the bitch did to my soldier) would be the thinking man's reasoning.

Fenton and Osmond looked away as Rudd eased the shirt from Miles's chest. In doing so, he allowed to escape the odor of Miles which, to all but the filthiest vermin, would cause at the very least a momentary turn of the head, but not so with Rudd whose senses had long ago become indifferent to any effluvium but that of a saucy stinging waft of scotch. Jill emerged from the ladies' room and approached Rudd and Miles with a pitcher of water (which she had noticed a disturbing yellow tinge in—not as it came from the tap but as it accumulated in the glass pitcher) and some paper towels. They all watched with not a small amount of awe as she wiped Miles's shoulder (to little avail as the bleeding was very bad) and put her lips to his much-torn flesh and sucked quickly and effectively that bullet from him. Miles answered with a reflex and scream that sent Jill tumbling back, gasping for air while puking bullet and blood and whatever else. So Jill was forgiven even though the initial outrage—it would be termed in another reality—was somewhat superficial. Miles *had* endangered their safety (liquor, which was all their safety had ever amounted to) and not once but twice. Nothing was said. But this event had sobered them and more drinking was in order. Amen.

This momentary peace (albeit internal and somewhat uncertain) was to come to an end and, even before the busboy first recognized the bombings as something more significant than the routine gunfire and firefights, the tiniest shaking of the earth around Tony's began to have its effect on forty-some menisci in dry-storage, which began to barely oscillate. The irony of the increasingly insistent molotov cocktails was not lost on Rudd, who recognized the homemade firebombs' nearness by the subtle sloshing of his own scotch well. The explosions were somewhere very near the rear of the building, maybe the homes just behind the parking lot? The increasing trembling of the pots and utensils was nothing compared to that of the busboy, who had taken cover under a prep table when several of the bombs hit near enough to start those quakings.

Jill, finally shaken by the rumblings, emerged from the bathroom where she had been since administering her Last Blow (suck) Job. Rudd stood, with a definite feeling of panic. He looked at Jill, who would be the only one he could count on for real help now with Langston still passed out and no doubt near DTs upon re-entry and Miles shot and the busboy hating him. Fenton and Osmond maybe help but Jill help good.

"I could sure use you right now," he said to her, really meaning it and her ears lit up. Being used was something she was good at and enjoyed. "I have to trust you now Jill. I'll get Langston and Miles under cover and you go to dry-storage and check things out." He felt a need to stay with the men and surely the basement of this place would stand up to anything, although he felt an uneasy chuckle approach when he almost wished this was L.A. 'cause there the buildings were built to withstand an earthquake for chrissake but L.A. was no doubt nothing but a mere cinder by now.

Jill hesitated for a moment then, realizing she was part of the team, reluctantly recruited at that but a part nonetheless, she turned and made her way to dry-storage. She plodded down the steps thinking that things seemed pretty solid. She grabbed a flashlight and

at that moment Osmond rose from his stool and headed for the men's room. The previous bombings shook him up, shook him bad but not like this Osmond thought as he opened the stall door and entered dry-storage. There was some motion here but that was to be expected there had been bombs before that had caused, well, hell the whole building to be

pulled from behind the commode a full-new-as-you-please-seal-intact bottle of 151 Ronrico Dark Rum, the very one he had

rattled about and this was, after all, a basement. Jill squinted as the flashlight gave little help in the far corners of the tiny once adequate now inadequate room where things seemed to be okay as far as Jill could see but she would faithfully report her findings to the Captain. Had Jill's eyes been

appropriated from dry-storage not an hour before and caressed it in the dark, enjoying its soon to be lost virginity. The glass of the bottle was inviting and dangerous like an armed woman. Osmond cracked the seal, pausing to enjoy the slight tearing sound, and reverently raised the bottle to his lips. He kissed it and it engulfed him, swallowing him further with each gluttonous swill.

those of a hard-core drunk, perhaps she would have been more concerned, more inclined to ensure the bottles were shielded, protected by some barrier that would heroically defend them from any harm. But this was not the case so Jill, satisfied that all was well (well, kinda funny cause dry-storage was like a real well, like well liquor), turned heel and headed back up the stairs.

Jill and Osmond returned to the bar, Osmond back to his booth with a half bottle of Ronrico hidden beneath a towel and poorly at that but the others were too preoccupied (with bombs and bottles) to notice, and Jill with news.

"How is it?" Fenton. Rudd looking too.

"A little shaky, but no worse than before, I think it'll hold—barring any serious shit." Jill being honest, helpful.

Fenton and Rudd had managed to drag Langston to his booth which seemed as safe as anywhere and Miles the same. The latter had been plied with much alcohol, painkiller now (an excuse they all had used at one time or another before such self-serving apologies became too transparent and wasn't it ironic that now that very excuse was bona fide) and was nearly passed out from its intake as much as the concurrent blood loss. Osmond, in his booth now sat still, staring at the door. There was a brief threatening moment of quiet.

The bombs began again more insistent now. They continued for what would be in real-time about a half hour, and for Fenton and Rudd it was their finest hour. Renegade heroes defending the castle and its cache. Jill too, returning fire, shooting the unseen bad guys. So taken were they with this gallery and the role playing within it that when Fenton looked to Rudd and queried, "Dry-storage?" Rudd's response, drunken and exhilarated came, "Better a few less bottles than one less man. I need more than Jill for return fire and the others aren't with me like you." Rudd allowed himself to puff slightly at his own Rightness. John Wayne now, my men first.

So Rudd Did What He Had To Do and in doing so, became gravely uncomfortable with his own self-inflicted bravado. And Rudd and Fenton and Jill returned fire and Langston remained passed out which bothered Rudd 'cause this was one hell of a ruckus. Miles passed in and out of consciousness, whatever that was, but managed to contribute a few shots. Rudd doubted his targets were real and thought he would be better off unarmed but let it go. Osmond was in the can, scared—literally—shitless no doubt, throughout the attack, only to emerge at its conclusion and pass out (die) in his booth. The forty-some menisci continued to dance, with more vigor now and they were presently joined by the shelving, which bounced just a bit, keeping rhythm, making dry-storage a considerably lively (deadly) place indeed.

Day17

It is dawn at Tony's. All of its denizens sleep. For Jill and the busboy, it is a natural state or as natural a state as one could hope for in this oh-so-unnatural New World. For the others it is a stygian blackness from which nightmarish demons issue forth, threatening them, taunting them, We'll get you, we'll get you. And of course they will. Even those malicious vendors of fate are dwarfed by the terror at the bottom of an empty bottle. Sleep. Some intermission.

The damage to this worthy fortress is severe. Fubarr-ed, Rudd would have deemed the situation in his decidedly tran-spired youth. Wait for the curious looks before revealing the acronym, "You know—*fubarr-ed:* fucked up beyond all rea-sonable repair!" The boys would snicker and exchange furtive acknowledgments, conspiratorial with the mention of the "f" word. That game is long ago and the danger here is imminent although not in the traditional sense but in the sense that there's precious few drops of liquor here and the prospect of finding more on the other side of that door is nothing more than pathetic. Concerning that door, there is almost nothing left of the exterior shutters. The interior shutters are wildly specked with holes through which the sun is spitting tubes of yellow light. Tony templetomb hurt bad. Mortality showing and hangin' out all over the place.

The busboy sleeps just outside of the door leading to dry-storage where he had taken shelter the evening before. He is kept company by broken glass and the sweet perfume smell of booze, all that's left really, the source of the seductive scent long gone now. Jill is in the restroom, filling her last sanctuary with restless dreams whose only residue will be a troubling feeling of fear and a sheath of perspiration. The bartender continues to decay in the unfrozen freezer. Osmond, not nearly as far along in his own death, lies on the floor of the booth where he expired, organs and blood still infused with Ronrico perhaps retarding the rotting of his flesh. The front of his shirt still reeks of the 151 which left a telling stain—the very one his brothers-at-arms discovered upon rolling over his body to confirm his death and betray its real cause. That disclosure, in turn led all parties to unite and agree upon the dead man's eternal status as a sonofabitch (envy, not anger, was what moved them to this judgment and they all knew it but this remained unsaid amongst them just the same). For Rudd, Fenton, Miles, and Langston; livers enlarge to unprecedented proportions, wounds fester and noxious breath continues in and out of the miasma that fills the interior of their lungs. So it is not that goodnight (badnight?), not yet at least. Yet.

Such is the scene that the bullet-induced sunbeams illuminate. Their light does not reach the five plastic juice containers that are resting at the base of the bar's interior, beneath the scrubber sink. It is here that the entire treasury of liquor now resides. Utilizing the plastic bottles is the result of a unanimous (unanimous among Rudd and Fenton, the others being either unavailable or unimportant) decision to transfer all remaining liquor to the less delicate vessels after the evening's attacks had subsided. It is here they rest and here they contain:

1. One complete fifth of Malinowa Raspberry Cordial Austrian Liqueur.
2. One complete fifth of J&B.
3. The remnants of what was left in the recently shot bottle of J&B combined with the small amount left in Langston's DT bottle. babygottabottlebabygottabottle.
4. One complete bottle of the dry-storage salvage blend.
5. Half a bottle of the same (the original amount had been lightened by Rudd who at some point during the night swigged enough to stave off the impending withdrawals. Rudd.).

They had made it (if that's what it could be called and surely it was the only thing it could be called—*made* not in the manufacturing sense, but in the sense that they made their lives last for those hours, no small accomplishment for these men) through the night. It is at this juncture that Langston's screams begin to pepper the what would otherwise be dewy morning. Jill, already awake in the restroom, hurries to enter the bar but not before ensuring each of the three hooks and eyes of her bra are securely fastened. Oops, missed one, there we go. Okay now.

There is sufficient light for her to get an eyeful of her patient who is wailing and writhing, sightless eyes rolled over white to the back of his head. In between nonsensical screams, Langston sucks on a chard of glass that had been discarded after its contents had been so carefully (albeit shakily) decanted into one of the plastic juice containers. Blind Delirious Man Sniffs Out Liquor on Glass Chard, the headlines would read. The glass has lacerated his lips and tongue. To what extent is difficult to judge as blood covers most of the bottom half of his face and a small river of that same blood and saliva is making its way down his chin.

Jill thought she could handle anything and she will handle this. Just gimme a second. A second, a moment. Maybe a lifetime. She steadies herself as the freakish scene causes her own blood to drain from her face, a faintish feeling upon her. For the first time she is shook, really shook by the magnitude of the Evil these men define their souls upon. And they are all she has.

"Jesus Christ Jill, get a bottle. JeSUS CHRIST NOW," Rudd staring at her wondering why she hasn't moved and feeling not too far behind Langston at that. Jill snaps from her own private and terrible shock and assumes her role (surely this must be playacting) once again. She scurries behind the bar and clutches the first container her hand encounters. Unfortunately, it is the Raspberry Cordial and that—being only seventy-six proof—is not the best choice given the problem. Not best but okay in the it'll-do sense.

"Here now," Jill kneels by Langston (not too close) and Rudd approaches him from behind. "I'll grab his arms.

You hold his head with one hand and pour what you can with the other."

Jill takes a firm hold of Langston's head and is surprised how vulnerable he feels in her arms. She cuts herself as she grabs the glass and removes it from Langston's lips, slicing him there even further. Now, her blood mingles with Langston's. Jill. The bottle. She manages to get about three-quarters of what she pours into him. Langston finds that little comfort and subsides into minor spasms. Quiet.

Rudd and Jill step away with a lets-see-how-that-works expression on their faces. Kids in a chemistry lab regarding their recently concocted experiment as it bubbles in the beaker before them. There is blood everywhere now, its thick scent heady and ominous. Rudd, his own shakes becoming apparent, grabs the nearly empty (but hard to tell since its contents are cloaked with a coating of blood on the bottle's exterior) container from Jill and drains it. Funny, he thinks, this Raspberry Cordial shit ain't so bad. Jill watches this and it kindles the unlikely memory of a thirsty athlete in a television ad, swigging down his sports drink. "Quenches deep down!" he would say. Commercial smile and all.

The others are awake and on the scene, eyes downcast in embarrassment. Miles, Fenton, and Rudd take their seats at the bar.

"I think it's best we dole the rest out according to need," Rudd.

"Which means what? You get the most? Langston? You know I've got some serious pain here." Patting his shoulder, Miles.

What an asshole. Rudd looks poker-face level at Miles. Guy's trying to play ordinary rules.

"I think it's getting a little too close to the surface for this kind of shit Miles. Now Fenton here isn't likely to go down. We all know that, but he's been here and he's stood by us, so he deserves a share. Fenton, how about you get the half bottle of mash. We'll use the full bottle of mash on Langston over here. Miles and I can split the remaining J&B."

Fenton opens his mouth in protest then thinks better of it. After all, this is where we're at and there's nothing else left to do. Miles is quiet too, what with Rudd agreeing to divvy up the J&B. Fair's fair. It had to come to an end, that much they knew. They regard this . . . this *end* as men facing their own death, marooned derelicts splitting the last bits of food, any hope of rescue long gone, starvation imminent. They sit together, still for a moment. Still except for the random gunfire, which they have all but ceased to care about.

Rudd, not forgetting his obligations now, "Come on, we better sit on the floor, or at least the booths, there's no telling what could penetrate now. Fenton, bring the bottles around. Jill, let's see what we can do for Langston."

Fenton goes behind the bar and retrieves the four bottles, handing the full mash to Jill, he sets the half mash by his booth and unscrews the tops on the J&Bs to even them out. He begins to pour from the fuller bottle to the less full bottle when the shake in his hands forces him to abort the attempt. He is reluctant to draw attention to this at the same time aware that he has little choice.

"Jill," Fenton, voice quaking, "I can't do it."

Jill turns to see him helpless, holding out his hands that are quivering with that involuntary palsy she has become so familiar with.

"I'll be right there, let me see about him first." She responds, nodding toward Langston who is still somewhat calm from the earlier ministrations. Having fetched some wet paper towels (and now the water from the tap is starting to smell, really smell) Jill cradles Langston's head in her lap and dabs blood from his face. He drinks nearly a quarter of the bottle in a greedy, sloppy fashion. Jill recaps the bottle and sets it next to the seat on the floor of his booth. She walks to the bar and rations out the J&B between the two bottles. Her work done for now, she returns to the restroom to clean up.

The men sit, guns and liquor placed finite before them. This eventuality now coming to fruition. Each with his own exclusive set of truths. Never more alone. There is random firing on the door, and Rudd or Fenton answers it, still obeying the rules. Rudd is amused by this instinctive call to order. In this predictable faction, Rudd is the Lord of the Flies and they all know it. And not just know but *respect* it. Respect me, Dad, my men. But that's over now and Rudd accepts that. His last shred of morality is what brought them to this. Morality that has no home in this nihilistic New World. It was this that accelerated the end of the booze. Hardly what was called for, yes, but his last defining, albeit cataclysmic, gesture was enough for Rudd. His eyes drift to his thigh, the singular puncture there. So even a bullet could be incompetent. Why did it have to be the one meant for him? Selfish still.

But he knows that bottle he compulsively squeezes, now with both hands. It's his and his alone. It is the last bottle, just as they all have been. It is everything I have always been. Now the end he always knew loomed in his future was here. The end of the liquor, all the booze in the world always had an end. Drunks' paradise; holed up in a bar with all the booze you could want and even that had an end. Like drinking the last drop of water on the earth, or breathing the last breath of air, Rudd regards this last dose of scotch that way. He gazes at the bottle and watches as his hands now meld into the plastic, making it part of him. The hallucination speaks to him. Divided we fall.

"I'm sorry," he says aloud to no one, to everyone.

And really, no one does hear it, including Jill as she sits on the floor of the restroom assessing the situation. Run fingers through the thick pile carpet, helps thinking. Uh-oh, change hands, that hand leaves blood stains and that's a no-no. Think now. Stupid, Stupid, Stupid. Stupid men. Always leaving. Mindlessly spreading their seed and leaving. Tears begin to sting her eyes and she blinks them back. She is hot, confused, and angry. She licks the barrel of the Beretta, a supplication. This act offers no solace.

She enters the kitchen and sees the busboy there. He looks at her, aroused by her image. Breasts. Shirt wet with blood. Gun. Lips. Lips. Girl sets gun on table.

"Jose," she whispers the alias. This prompts a smirk from the busboy and he even considers telling her his real name. What could matter now? But he quickly abandons the idea.

"Come with me, follow me," she speaks to him in a low voice. Close to him, she reaches for his penis, another penis. The busboy responds to her and when they reach the ladies' room, his smirk has widened to a toothy grin and he even relaxes a bit as she performs a matter-of-fact striptease. She stands naked in front of the sink, visible only by the scant light filtered through the door and bullet-decayed window shutters.

"Go out now, see what you can find—more liquor maybe, help, guns, anything—and this is yours, whenever and however you want it." Jill eases herself onto the vanity and opens herself to him.

Busboy, busyboy now frees his erection and approaches Jill, thinking how he'd thought it would be easy, but not this easy. He gropes her breasts and bites at them. His erection is insistent though and he doesn't notice her dryness (or wet tears) as he pushes into her and begins an unpracticed, masturbatory thrusting.

Jill bears it, this will be over soon. God let it be over. She clenches her teeth, her eyes squeeze tears. The door opens and Rudd absorbs the scene. The busboy, grunting, climaxing. Rudd and Jill see each other.

"No, no," Jill, whimpering. Rudd lets the door swing shut. Yeah. That was Jill.

The busboy finishes and extracts himself from her. He wipes himself with a paper towel and Jill gazes at him vacantly, her eyes still puffy but dry now. His semen oozes onto her thigh.

"You're in luck lady, just so happens I was on my way out anyway," he says to her as he zips his fly.

"And *you*, you are *sweeeeet*," he hisses at her while simultaneously pinching and pulling her nipples. He turns to leave her alone in the now desecrated ladies' room.

The busboy, renewed, prances through the kitchen and toward the door, noticing that although it's closed, it is unbolted. Wha-thefuck? he thinks as he crosses that threshold for the last time and enters the impossibly sunny day.

Fenton is vaguely aware of some activity in the back, the kitchen but acknowledges it as he does the shooting, without resolution. Instead, he is trying hard to resist taking a drink. Seated at the bar with the Glock and bottle arranged on the slate surface. He contemplates the two. It is hard to focus and all of his resources, both cerebral and physical are right here. He is frightened at how rapidly he was assimilated into this hell. Ever since he entered Tony's he played this character, for Rudd as much as himself and now that identity is disintegrating. Without it, he isn't sure what is left, nothing is the answer in the cards. Facing it is quite another thing, that kind of courage isn't easy to come by. Not much of a man, nope. What now. Next.

Jill's voice rescues him from that loath immersion.

"The busboy went out. I sent the busboy out for . . . for whatever." She was unable to say the obvious for fear that doing so would make Fenton's visibly deteriorated condition too public. Like mentioning the word (liquor, booze, juice, hooch, scotch, a rose by any other name) would pull the curtain back and reveal him. Ruin him. She would not.

"The busboy?" Fenton. Unstable now. Unsure whether he should feel hope at this new, dim prospect of more liquor. Neither Jill nor Fenton knows the busboy is dead, used as target practice for some marksman, shot in the back of the head, his race never revealed to his assailants and vice versa.

"Yeah, he just left. He'll be okay. He was the last time. Right? C'mon now, try to pull yourself together. Have a drink. I'll get it for you." Jill stands and pours him a shot glass of the mash. Comforting. Soothing.

"Here, drink it." Jill.

Fenton downs the shot and surveys the bar, fortified. Miles is hovering over Osmond's body, engrossed. Langston is on the floor of his booth, catatonic. Rudd's booth is vacant although Fenton cannot remember when or how this came to pass. He feels a bolt of fear at his friend's absence, his own inadequacies surfacing again. The vacancy at Rudd's booth summons Fenton's attention.

"Rudd?"

Jill and even Miles, looking too now. Jill races around. Panic. Panic. Dry-storage, kitchen. Panic, sweat. Breath fast, shallow. Men's room! Should have checked there first. Panic. No Rudd. Back to the bar. Miles and Fenton stand by Rudd's booth. The bottle, still containing a swallow of scotch, the Walther, and Glock lay surrendered upon the table there. It is clear this will have to suffice as Rudd's final statement. He is gone.

* * *

"it's okay, fenton, it's okay 'cause think about it. just think about it. busboy back any minute. any minute. and what about ossie over here, one fat sonabitch. lotta liquor to kill that fat son of a bitch. probably some 'ya know—left, left in his big fatass stomach. probably a lot. big fatass. and a one hundred fifty-one a lot of it, enough to kill him *and then some.*"

Afterword
October 15, 1995

I had a drink at Tony's the other day. Eighteen days ago to be exact. Eighteen days, that's one day longer than my friends at the other Tony's can even hope to plan for. Then again, living the eighteenth day is something I've taken for granted until now. The original Tony's, the one I stopped at, is still there under the same management as well as the same roof. This would be the one my brother, John O'Brien, worked at when he was about sixteen. I doubt it's changed much since 1976 and it's not a very tony place, as John described it on Day16. As far as Gail's concerned, well I suppose we'll never know. The authenticity of that part of the story is for the memories of John and the imaginary-or-not Gail.

I sat at the bar, drank some wine. Johnny was there too. Just a kid, hardworking, joking with the waitresses, bartender. Mid-afternoon, slow time at this place. Extra time to fool around and why not, everyone likes this kid. He really is a funny kid. Cracks everybody up. But, of course, Johnny wasn't there. Hasn't been there for almost twenty years. Hasn't been anywhere in going on two years. That's because he's dead now. Shot himself in April of 1994. Bye John.

But in another way, he's been here with me for every day of those barely eighteen months. Since his death, I've been reading his work and studying authors he favored. Yes, lately, it's been quite a John-a-thon for me. He'd have thought that was funny, *John-a-thon*, and maybe it was a lifetime ago. I read *The Assault on Tony's* just before that pilgrimage to the real Tony's. John last edited the documents associated with the novel twelve days before his suicide. The last passage in the book by John's hand was this one:

> For the first time in his life Rudd found himself wishing for death, hoping (praying?) that the walls came down before the liquor ran out, that they were stormed, bombed or shot in some truculent surprise attack, some irresistible force, divine intervention.

And then my brother died, or brought his own demise to fruition, which is a truer statement, however cloaked by silky words.

But his computer sits in the room next to where I sleep, or don't sleep. Who could with a dead man's unwritten words haunting them every night. So, armed with time, good intention, and John's blood in my veins, I set out to finish *Assault*. I should also mention that I had his outline. Instructions from the grave as it were. Yeah, John, I get it.

He had adhered to the outline pretty faithfully throughout the completed portion of the novel. Between his notes and my instinct, I knew, too painfully well, how it ended. He and I had always had a somewhat telepathic communication between us and it hasn't been lost these last days I've spent with *Assault*. Although there is a good amount of John's prose in the novel that was not in the outline, the main gist was there for me. From John's last words on is my embellishment of the end he had sketched out. Of course, this subject matter isn't easy and I apologize to the reader for my enormous ineptitude. John was an extremely talented writer, one of the gifted ones. His shadow is potent to say the least, and any ability I hope to have is dwarfed next to his, quite literally in this case. The only thing I can profess is that I'm certain this is how John would have ended the novel. Of course, his signature is missing from the prose. But I make no apologies regarding subject matter. John's world was a gritty one. To put a hopeful twist on the fate of our unfortunate crew at Tony's would be preposterous, unthinkable.

I have robbed the reader of the "Bourbon and Bile" joke John alludes to in his notes, only because I don't know it. Simultaneously, I saved the same John's gruesome proposal to end the novel with Miles and Fenton going to work on Osmond with a knife. And this only because John *allowed* me to by thankfully adding to that note, ". . . or darkly end the book by just considering it." I do appreciate that, big brother.

I have come to know Rudd, Carey, Fenton, Langston, Miles, Osmond, Jill, the busboy, and even the dead bartender very well. I'll spare the reader my abundant commentary on them and John's work in general. He does appear in the novel in a fragmented sense. He is the liberal part of Carey, the moralistic persuasion in Rudd, and he possessed the same profound addiction as Langston.

John was in Los Angeles during the riots in 1992 and relatively sober at that time. His wife happened to be in Cleveland on family business, and we were all worried about John living that frightening truth on the other side of the country. Of course, in John's mind he was living a part of history. The experience stayed with him. Riots loom in the background of *Better* (a yet unpublished novel by John) and have an integral part in *Assault*. I spoke to him during those tumultuous days back in 1992. He had bought a gun–the gun–a Smith & Wesson. He took out a lot of cash. Everyone should have to experience curfew at some point in life. Don't worry honey, I'm fine. Really I am, there's no trouble here in Venice Beach. I love you too.

John has left behind so much. He was a truly tragic character of our time. It's amazing how much I've learned from him. It sometimes makes me believe he isn't really dead at all, but with me here, sitting at his computer, helping me. I still use many of the programs that were originally installed by John. When I sign in to the word processing program I am reminded of this as "John O'Brien, me" blips on the screen.

John is gone now. The wound he left grows imperceptibly less painful with time. I live in apprehension of my thirty-fourth birthday, the day that I reach the age my big brother couldn't make it to. It is the day I will outgrow him, the day he will eternally become my little brother. Every piece of life I experience from that day on will be jaded in my own mind, characterized as one John never allowed himself. Such is the sentence passed upon those left behind by a suicide victim.

I'll see you, John O'Brien, me, when I sign in tomorrow. I hope I've made you proud and done what you would have wanted me to do.

Love, Erin